Kate N. Northup

1903 —

THE MONK
AND THE DANCER

THE MONK
AND
THE DANCER

BY
ARTHUR COSSLETT SMITH

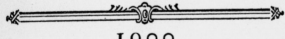

NEW YORK: CHARLES SCRIBNER'S SONS

1900

D. B. Updike, The Merrymount Press, Boston

"Khadija believes in me"

CONTENTS

THE MONK
AND THE DANCER

THE MONK
AND THE DANCER

I. LA TRAPPE

I

FOR three weeks, and well into Lent, the rain had fallen upon the thirsty soil of Algeria; then one night the wind shifted, and the next day the blazing sun rode through a cloudless sky.

At the abbey of La Trappe at Staouëli the monks hailed the coming of spring with joy. It meant for them the beginning of out-door work, the culture of the vines, the tending of the *nessri*, or white roses, from which they extract the attar, and the geraniums which furnish the essence for which the abbey is famous; it meant the herding of the cattle and the sheep in the outlying pastures, the songs of the birds in the hedges, the rustling of the grass; it meant the exchange of whitewashed cells for the open air and the blue sky.

Of the forty monks of La Trappe two only are permitted to speak; these are the Abbot and the guest-master, Brother Ambrose. The others may say "Memento mori" when they meet each morning, and may pray. Beyond this they are dumb. Each spends a few moments of the day in digging his own grave, and they sleep on straw, with their coffins for beds. On the wall of the refectory is this inscription: "*S'il est dur de vivre à la Trappe, qu'il est doux d'y mourir!*" Over each door is the word "*Silence.*"

Just outside the walls of the abbey, by the great gates, there is a room devoted to hospitality. Here each day, from ten to twelve o'clock, food is given to all who come. Brother Ambrose has charge of this room, and serves each guest with his own hands.

On this first morning of spring Brother Ambrose went to the Abbot and made a request.

[2]

"Father," he said, "this fine day after the long rain will bring many travellers, and I am beginning to feel my age. Will you kindly give me help?"

The Abbot thought a moment, then pointing through the open window toward the garden, he asked, "Who is that among the geraniums?"

Brother Ambrose shaded his eyes with his hand, and answered, "It is Brother Angelo. But is he not too young? There will be many guests, and," he added, "women as well as men."

The Abbot looked up quickly, a faint smile upon his lips.

"Ah, Brother Ambrose," he said, "at what age does one become safe? Send Brother Angelo to me."

The Abbot saw Brother Ambrose go down the grass walk toward the scarlet geraniums. Then he resumed his seat. Soon there was a knock at the door.

"Enter," said the Abbot. Brother Angelo came in.

"Memento mori, father," he said.

[3]

"I try to," replied the Abbot. Brother Angelo stared.

"My son," said the Abbot, "how long have you been with us?"

"Always, father."

"And how old are you, my son?"

"Twenty-two years, father."

The Abbot opened his desk and took out a small red book fastened with a lock. He selected a key from those which hung at his girdle and opened the book.

"My son," he said, "Brother Ambrose is growing old, and I have told him that you will help him. I intend that you shall take his place some day. For that reason you were taught languages. At present you are not to speak to any of the guests. Brother Ambrose will attend to that. Now listen to what I shall read to you, and ask no questions."

The Abbot turned several pages, and then read:

"'*Angelo, Brother. Born April second,* 1873. "*Baptized the same day and named Charles* "*Victor.*

"*Father, Count Charles François d'Apre-*
"*mont, Colonel of the Fourth Chasseurs*
"*d'Afrique.*
"*Mother, Miriam, an Almée woman of the*
"*tribe of Ouled Nail, who danced in the cafés*
"*of Biskra, and who died April third,* 1873.
"*Given to me May first,* 1873, *by his fa-*
"*ther, who in the world was my friend, and*
"*who died in the desert some time in May,*
"1873.
"*Took the final vows on Easter Monday,*
"1895.

"*Signed by me,* RICHARD,
"*Abbot of La Trappe.*'"

"I read you this, my son, for you are
going to-day outside of the protecting
walls, and are to catch a glimpse of the
world. Remember how little the world
has done for you. You owe it nothing but
life. You will pay your debt when you
die. Now go to Brother Ambrose."

At ten o'clock the guests began to
come. There were Spaniards from Oran,
Maltese from Bona and the Tunis frontier,
French peasants from the neighboring

farms, an Englishman or two, and a commercial traveller from Lyons. Brother Angelo scarcely noticed them. He did what Brother Ambrose bade him do: he found seats at the tables for the peasants and their families; he handed about the fish, the bread, the lentils, and the cheese; he comforted a crying child; he served the wine, and all the while he was saying to himself, "My father was Count d'Apremont, and my mother was Miriam, the dancing-girl of Biskra."

Just before twelve o'clock, when all the guests except an Englishman and the commercial traveller had departed, a carriage stopped at the gate; and a moment after the door opened, and a woman, followed by a courier belonging to one of the hotels at Algiers, entered the room. She turned, startled by the cheerless appearance of the place, and was about to go out, when her eyes met those of Brother Angelo; then she walked slowly to the head of the table and took her seat. The courier sat at the foot. Brother Ambrose served her, and she made a pretence of eating. She cast occasional glances at the young monk, and he never took his eyes away from her. He stood staring at what he had never seen before—a beautiful woman.

She was very dark. Her hair was blue-black, twisted into a heavy knot at the back of her head, and over her ears two sharply pointed locks curved up like sickles on her temples. She wore a little black hat, such as Spanish bull-fighters wear, tilted down upon her brows. Her nose was straight and thin, pinched in just above the nostrils, which quivered with each breath. Her lips were full and red, and her white teeth were small and shaped like orange seeds. Her hands were those of the old races, with long pointed fingers and rosy nails. She wore a dozen rings, and all were set with emeralds. Once she looked about the room, and saw the Englishman and the commercial traveller; afterward she did not notice them.

[7]

When she could no longer make a pretence of eating she turned to Brother Ambrose and said, "You have an excellent white wine here, I am told. May I not taste it?"

"Why not?" replied Brother Ambrose, and off he went to bring a bottle from the abbey cellars.

Scarcely had the door closed behind him, when she turned and looked fairly at Brother Angelo. He stood as before, tall and lithe, his closely cut hair curling about his face, his black eyes sparkling, his cheeks glowing, his full lips parted, his hands pressed upon his breast.

"Come here," she said.

He took a step toward her.

"What is your name?" she asked.

He started, and put his finger to his lips.

She laughed, put her hands to her lips, and threw him a kiss.

"What is your name?" she repeated.

"Memento mori," he gasped.

"How droll!" she said. "That sounds

like Latin, and I do not know Latin. I only know my own language, and the French which I am using. It is not good French. My accent is very bad. You remind me of a picture I saw in Florence. It was of a young man into whom they had shot arrows. I think they called him Saint Sebastian. I see that you wear sandals. That is good; it gives one a carriage. The Arabs wear sandals, and they walk properly. I also wear no heels," and she put out her little feet. "In the evening, if I wear slippers, then heels—in the daytime, no. That is so that I may walk well. I sent the old man for the wine so that I might speak to you. He looks rather cross, but then he is old. It is very sad to be old. I am twenty. I have nearly ten years yet. Then I shall marry. It seems that you are not talking much, but you are blushing very nicely. I used to blush when men spoke to me. It is a very pretty accomplishment, but I have lost it. Still, if you will come to see me at the Hotel Saint George, I will try my best to recall it. Will you come? If you intend to say something nice to me, or to kiss my hand, you must do it very soon, before the old man returns with the wine."

"Mademoiselle," said the courier, "pray be careful. The Abbot is very strict."

"This Abbot," she said, with a laugh, "if one could only know, is probably nothing but a man."

Then she turned to Brother Angelo again, and whispered, "What is your name?"

The blood left his face, and he trembled like a leaf. Then he said, "My father was Count d'Apremont, and my mother was Miriam, the dancing-girl of Biskra." And he burst into tears.

There was a crash. Brother Ambrose stood in the door, and he had dropped the bottle of white wine.

The Englishman and the commercial traveller walked down the road together. "Monsieur," said the latter, "she is almost better in real life than on the stage."

"Very clever," said the Englishman. "Who is she?"

The commercial traveller stopped short, and looked hard at his companion. Finally he said, "Is it possible that monsieur does not know? She is Dolores, the Spanish dancer. They pay her two thousand francs a night at the Folies-Bergères."

II

THAT evening, when Brother Ambrose had made his report, the Abbot sat silent for some moments, and then said, "You are quite sure that he spoke?"

"Quite sure, father."

"And to a woman?"

"To a woman, father," and Brother Ambrose crossed himself.

"Was she an attractive person?"

"She was as handsome as the devil."

The Abbot looked up quickly, but Brother Ambrose was evidently sincere in his comparison.

"Yes," he continued, "in all the thirty years that I have been guest-master I have never seen one like her. When she walked up the room she seemed to float along; there was no movement of her skirts. There was a faint odor of violets about her that filled the air. She had a fashion of half closing her eyes and looking at you through the lashes. There was that picture of the repentant Magdalen which Brother Thomas painted last year, and which you bade him burn, because, although it was the Magdalen, it was not repentant. Well, this woman had that same look. Her throat—"

"That will do," said the Abbot, "I understand."

The two old men looked at each other silently. Then Brother Ambrose, shifting his feet and nervously fingering the beads of his rosary, said, "Father, when the spring comes back, when the whole earth begins to breathe again, when the starlings build their nest in the great cross on the chapel roof, and the scent of the lilacs fills the air, do you never find 'memento mori' hard words to say?"

The Abbot went to the window, looked out, came back, and said slowly, "Brother Ambrose, on such a night as this, after the manner of men, I fight with beasts at Ephesus."

"Thank God," said Brother Ambrose, solemnly, "that I am not the only one. And now, father," he added, briskly, "what is to be done with Brother Angelo?"

"You may put him in the chapel cell for to-night," replied the Abbot, "and in the morning I will fix his penance. You may leave him his straw, and bring me the key of the cell."

"Is that all?" asked Brother Ambrose.

"Yes," replied the Abbot.

Brother Ambrose started for the door.

"Memento mori, father," he said.

The Abbot smiled.

"I will grant you an indulgence to-night, old friend. Good night."

Brother Ambrose's lips quivered.

"Good night," he said. And then he added, "Those words sound very sweet after thirty years."

In ten minutes he brought the key of the chapel cell, and the Abbot fastened it to his girdle.

Brother Ambrose lingered a moment, and then said, "If it is permitted, father, I should like you to say good night once more."

"Good night," said the Abbot, and then Brother Ambrose went away.

Left alone, the Abbot sat unconsciously playing with the keys at his waist, then rising, he extinguished the single candle upon his desk, and opening his door, stepped out upon the grass walk.

The garden was bathed in moonlight. On the long lines of almond trees the white blossoms shone like silver stars. High on the chapel roof the great iron cross was silhouetted against the sky, and the Abbot could see, at the intersection of the arms, the starling's nest. He walked slowly on past the geraniums, their scarlet flowers black in the moonlight, and then he came to the roses. All about him were the bending stems, the delicate, fresh leaves, and the great, white flowers. He circled with his arms a dozen of the stalks, brought them close together, and buried his face in the mass of blossoms. He breathed in the fragrance with long gasps ; and then, after a moment, he went on down the grass walk. At the corner of the wall was a stone bench, upon which the leaves of the vines cast delicate shadows. Here he took his seat. Behind him, trellised on the wall, was a mass of honeysuckle and jasmine, the perfume of which saturated the warm air. From the dovecote came the soft cooing of the pigeons, and in the far-off fields he heard the lowing of the cattle, for even the birds and the beasts felt the sweet influence of the spring, and could not sleep.

The Abbot sat motionless for a moment, overwhelmed by the beauty of the night, then suddenly he threw himself upon his knees.

"O God," he sobbed, "help thy servant!"

When he rose, an hour later, his prayer had been answered, and a sweet smile played about his lips.

"I will do it this very night," he said to himself, and then he went swiftly up the grass walk. He did not enter his own room, but passed through the cloisters to a door near the chapel wall. He opened this door, went in, and closed it after him. He was then in a small passage which led to the barred door of the chapel cell. It was perfectly dark, but the Abbot put his hand on the wall and felt his way to the end of the passage.

"My son?" he whispered.

There was no answer, but the Abbot heard a rustling in the straw.

"My son," he said, his voice trembling, "what I read to thee this morning was all true, except that thy father did not die in the desert. He is alive and is here. I am Charles François d'Apremont. I am thy father."

[16]

There was no reply.

The Abbot put his hands upon the barred door, and it swung open. The lock was broken. With a cry he entered the cell. He felt the straw under his feet, and he heard a rat scamper out into the passage. The cell was empty.

The Abbot went quickly out through the cloisters, across the wide courtyard, where the fountain was casting jets of silver in the moonlight, and on down the paved walk to the great gates. He found them locked and barred as usual; but as he was turning away, he saw projecting from the shadow of the further gate-post the foot of a ladder. Then his heart failed him utterly, for he knew that he had lost his son.

He went slowly to the ladder, and tripping on his robe, he mounted step after step, until he could see the world surrounding the great wall which for more than twenty years had bounded his horizon.

He saw the white road stretching away

to Algiers, and the long lines of eucalyptus trees which bordered it and cast their
shadows across it. He saw cultivated fields
and patches of woodland, and far off in
the distance he caught the twinkle of a
light in the window of a shepherd's hut.
As he gazed at these things, so strange
and yet so well known, there surged from
his heart to his mind the memories of the
world. He saw himself at the head of his
regiment; he heard the neighing of the
horses, and he saw the glint of the moonlight on the sabres and the buckles; he
heard the bugles; he saw the fierce skir-
mish in the desert; he saw the mosques
and the citadel of Biskra; and then—
ah, then he saw Miriam the dancing-girl
coming to meet him under the palm trees.

He waved his hand toward the distant
city, and whispered, "Farewell, my son!
God keep thee!"

I

IT was ten o'clock when Brother Angelo stepped from the ladder to the coping of the wall, hung by his hands for an instant, and then dropped softly into the world.

He knew four languages, his breviary, and how to tend geraniums; otherwise he was as much a child as when, twenty-two years before, an officer of the Chasseurs had brought him in his arms to La Trappe and the great gates had closed upon them both.

But his ignorance did not occur to him as he shortened his robe on one side to the knee and started down the moonlit road toward Algiers. He walked smoothly and swiftly, like the Arabs, with his head held high and his arms swinging easily. In two hours he came to Sidi Ferruch, and as he passed the barracks a sentinel called from the shadow of the gate, "*Qui vive?*"

[19]

"Memento mori," replied Brother Angelo, and passed swiftly on. Soon he came to the lighthouse of Cape Caxine and for the first time saw the sea and heard the clamor of the surf. Then he passed the old Moorish fort at Point Pescade, and further on, he went through Saint Eugène, where the villas stood white and silent in the moonlight.

It was two o'clock in the morning when he reached Mustapha Supérieur and saw the lights of the city and harbor beneath him. He had made the eighteen miles in four hours, and turning off from the road, he lay down under a mimosa tree to wait for the lazy sun.

About six o'clock the concierge of the Hotel Saint George came out of the side entrance, looked up to the sky, stretched his arms, yawned, and kicked a dog that came to greet him. Soon the courier who had been at La Trappe the preceding day joined him.

"How is mademoiselle?" asked the concierge.

"Well enough," replied the courier, "but I am glad to be through with her. Yesterday she made a fool of a young monk at the monastery, and Brother Ambrose caught him at it. It's a chance if they let me in the next time I go. Such as she spoil business. She pays well, but I am glad that she is leaving. She takes the steamer this evening for Naples."

"Her maid tells me," said the concierge, "that she has made fools of many. A bull-fighter in Seville was the first one. He started her. Then she took to dancing and the men flocked after her. They say the Prince of—"

"Mother of Heaven!" exclaimed the courier, "Here's the monk."

Brother Angelo came swiftly up the driveway, a mass of yellow mimosa blossoms in his hand.

"I have arrived," he said to the courier.

"So I perceive," replied the latter.

"Where is she?" asked Brother Angelo.

"She is where I should be if the world

were rightly managed," said the courier; "she is in bed."

"Is she ill? It is past six o'clock."

Just then a buxom young woman came onto the terrace.

"There is her maid," replied the courier; "ask her."

For the second time in his life Brother Angelo spoke to a woman.

"Tell me," he said eagerly, "is she ill? She told me to come, and I got over the wall while the rest were at complines. Will you not tell her that I am here?"

The young woman looked at him in silence.

"Perhaps," he said, "you do not understand French. I speak also Spanish, English, and Arabic."

"You speak plainly enough," said the maid, "but I was wondering what there was for me in all this. The little Jew chocolate-maker in Paris gave me fifty napoleons for one of mademoiselle's old slippers. The English milord used to pay postage in gold for every note I delivered, and the Abbé Guilbert gave me absolution and a kiss each time I let him in at the servants' door. What will you offer? We leave this evening, so I am obliged to speak frankly. What will you give?"

"Alas," said Brother Angelo, "I have nothing in the world but these," and he held out the mimosa blossoms.

"It is not business," said the maid, after a pause, "but perhaps you will make it up to me later," and snatching the flowers from his hands, she ran into the house.

Presently she came out again and whispered, so that the concierge should not hear her, "I put the flowers where she will be sure to see them. I will let you know when she wakes. It will be several hours yet. Go down by the fountain in the garden and wait for me."

She looked at him fixedly for a moment and said, "So you climbed the wall, did you? Good, that is the kind she likes." Then going, she turned her head and added, "That is the kind that all women like."

Brother Angelo went down the terrace into the garden and after some search found the fountain, which was hidden among the trees. He loosened his robe at the throat, turned it back, and plunged his head into the cold water. He took off his sandals and bathed his feet, and then, fresh and glowing, his crisp hair curling even more closely about his temples, he began to wait. Just then a neighboring clock struck seven, and unconsciously he repeated the office of "prime." Every day since he could remember he had said those words at this hour, sometimes with tears, sometimes with reverent joy, always with his whole heart. But that was ages ago; nearly twenty-four hours; before he had seen her; before his prayers were turned from the worship of an invisible God to the adoration of a visible goddess. He thought of his broken vows without regret. Why had the Abbot and Brother Ambrose deceived him all these years? Why had they taught him that the world was something to hide away from? He

[24]

looked about him and saw that it was good. Why had they talked so much of divine love when human love was at their very gates? Why had they taught him four languages, but never a word fit to speak to the woman he was soon to see again?

He felt a hand upon his shoulder.

"Come," said the maid, "you are lucky. She is awake, and it is not yet nine o'clock."

He followed her through the garden to the side entrance. They went up one flight of stairs, and then she opened a door and motioned to him. He put his hands to his heart and entered. It was a sitting-room, draped and furnished in the Moorish fashion. A little table between the windows was covered with a white cloth and a breakfast service for two persons. There were some trunks in the room, and the disorder which denotes either a recent arrival or an early departure. On the floor lay a woman's glove. Brother Angelo picked it up. It was the first glove

[25]

he had ever seen, but he quickly divined
its use. He spread it upon his palm, smiled
at its littleness, and then, blushing like a
girl, raised it to his lips.

A faint noise startled him and he turned
quickly. The curtains of the door leading
to the next room were parted ; and between them, dressed in white, with yellow mimosa blossoms at her bosom, stood
Dolores.

"Count d'Apremont," she said, "you
do me great honor ;" and stepping forward she let the curtains fall behind her.

For a moment they stood silent, then
he said, "What is *your* name ?"

She put her finger to her lips, cast down
her eyes, and whispered, "Memento
mori."

"What is your name ?" he asked again.

"My mother," she replied, "was a
gypsy girl of Seville, and my father—
perhaps he was a peasant, perhaps he was
the king. I never asked. My name is a
sad one. It is Dolores."

"Dolores," he repeated ; "that is Spanish. I know Spanish, English, French, and Arabic."

"With all those languages," she said, "you have still much to learn."

Then she came close to him and began playing with his crucifix. He felt her breath upon his cheek.

"There is another language, still," she said softly.

"Italian?" he gasped.

"No," she whispered, "although that is very like it. The language that I mean has no name and no words, but it is universal;" and she put her arms about his neck and kissed his lips.

II

THEY wandered slowly north, through Italy, following the spring; and when they reached Venice, behold it was June.

When a man is twenty-two and has strength and health and all his hair and the woman he loves, it is difficult to be unhappy anywhere during the month of June. In Venice it is impossible. For thirty days nature demonstrates in Venice what the world would have been had the serpent not glided into Paradise. Then the timorous tourist has fled to Como or Lucerne; the gondoliers demand only their legal fare; the sacristan at St. Mark's shows you the turquoise cup for an Italian cigar, and even asks you to come again; the waiters in the Piazza do not forget to return your change; the Venetians move back to their front rooms, which have been occupied during the winter by Americans; the last Doge turns over in his tomb; the voice of the Englishman is stilled in the land; and summer has come.

As for Brother Angelo, he walked on air. It is a fine thing to be a baby of twenty-two, and to be in love with one's nurse. Dolores's kiss in the little room of the Hotel St. George was the beginning of life for him. At that moment there fell from his eyes "as it had been scales," and the world burst upon his sight. People, customs, architecture, pictures, music, the

[28]

landscape, and most of all, the children and the beggars touched him.

"Dolores," he used to say, "here is a man who is hungry. Give him something."

And she would shrug her shoulders and say, "My friend, three months ago you had never tasted meat, and this man ate it this morning;" and then she would open her purse.

Music moved him strangely. Whether it was an organ in the street, a military band in the Piazza, or the Pope's choir at St. John Lateran, he used to stand entranced. Dolores would grow impatient.

"If you wish to hear music," she said, "you should hear the Tunisians in the elephant at the Moulin Rouge."

At Naples he had exchanged his monk's robe for the ordinary dress of a traveller.

"It is better so," said Dolores. "It is very *chic* for a great lady to have her private chaplain, but for *me* to travel with one—it is better so."

Nevertheless, when he first presented

himself in his new attire she put her hands over her eyes.

"Oh," she cried, "the romance has all gone out of it. You are now like everybody else, except," she added, "your eyes. They save you."

She bade him keep his monk's dress. "It will serve as a domino for the carnival masquerades," she said.

Rome wearied her.

"But, monsieur," she said to the guide who was conducting them through the Forum, "these buildings are very shabby, and all the people you are telling us of are dead. Is there no life in Rome, no *café-chantant*, no ballet?"

"There are the marionettes," he replied sullenly.

"Good," she cried, clapping her hands. "You will take a box for us for this evening."

"This evening!" exclaimed the guide, "This evening, madame, they illuminate the Coliseum and Professor Boldini delivers a lecture in the arena."

[30]

"How charming!" said Dolores; "but still you will take the box."

"There are people," she said to Angelo in Spanish, "who prefer the Coliseum to the marionettes. This is a strange world. There was an English milord who came to Seville to see me dance. He could stay but two days and the last was Sunday, and Juan was there, the greatest matador in Spain, and they killed eight bulls and fourteen horses, and one of the banderilleros was tossed so that he could never walk again. It was superb. And where do you think was milord all this while? In the Museum, looking at the Murillos! Oh, those English! They are cold. But," she added, "he gave me this ring—no, that one—Juan gave me this. Juan discovered me. Do you know what that means?" and she looked him full in the face.

"Of course you do not," she said. "I am constantly forgetting that you are only three months old."

Then, with a laugh, she added, "and

[31]

baby shall not see the naughty Coliseum; he shall see the pretty marionettes."

But if Rome wearied her, Venice was a delight.

The night that they arrived they sat in the little garden of the Hotel Britannia, close to the stone steps which lead down to the Grand Canal. Across the water, outlined by the moonlight, rose Santa Maria della Salute. To the left of the church, in the canal St. Mark, lay a schooner yacht, her harbor lights brightly shining. Off to the right were the dark masses of the Palace Esterhazy and the Academy. High above them hung the summer moon, sending a ladder of silver across the ripples of the lagoon to their very feet. They sat silent, her hand in his.

Presently, the soft, warm breeze brought the sound of music, and from behind the palaces on their left there came a gondola hung with colored lanterns and wreaths of flowers. It floated silently on until it was abreast of the little garden; then it stopped and, after a prelude by the violins and flutes, a woman began to sing the "*Si tu ne m'aimes pas*" from "Carmen." The laughter on the balconies and in the gondolas suddenly ceased; the sailors on the yacht, who were hoisting in the launch, stopped and belayed; the ripples against the stone steps seemed to hush and die away, and the very air hung breathless.

The song ceased, and for a minute there was perfect silence; then from the gondolas came shouts of "Calvé! Calvé!" which the shores took up until the palaces echoed back her name.

Dolores started to her feet. "Ah!" she exclaimed, "those cries are sweet to her. The finest thing in all this world is applause. I live on it, and I am famishing."

Then she came up to him and said, "Do you regret?"

"What?" he asked.

"Your broken vows—your chance of heaven."

"Heaven?" he said. "I have it now."

[33]

She shrugged her shoulders and put out her hands. "Why do you not tell the truth, you men, when women ask you questions? Why did you not say, 'Yes, I do regret'? Then I should have loved you; but you are all alike — milord, the chocolate-maker, the Abbé, the prince — you are all liars, except Juan. He was a man."

She snatched at her sleeve and pulled it up to her shoulder, her rounded arm shining like ivory in the moonlight.

"There," she cried, pointing to a red line above the elbow, "I was rolling a cigarette for Juan and I spilled the tobacco on the floor. His knife was on the table, and he did that. He was a man." And she bent her head and kissed the scar.

She walked rapidly up and down the terrace, humming the song that had so moved her. Then she stopped before him and said, "I am sorry that I spoke those words. You do not understand such things. How should you? Nevertheless, they were true. Women like me need the stick. We kiss the hand that strikes us.

We prefer an order to a request. Strength, audacity, force, a kiss and a blow, those are the things we like. A man must keep us women on our knees. If he lets us up we are apt to walk away. Even you, my friend, if it were not for your beauty, might in time grow monotonous. You never contradict me. You treat me as if I were a saint rather than a woman. If I touch your hand I feel you tremble. That is good. It is your French blood; but you are also half Arab and should know how to make me tremble. Arabs manage women and horses very well. They master them. The next time I ask anything of you, refuse it, will you?"

"I shall try to," he replied, wondering.

"Good," she said. "It will be refreshing. Now give me a kiss and end our quarrel."

"A hundred," he cried.

"You have forgotten already," she laughed.

"No," he said; "you asked for only one, and that I refuse."

She drew back and looked at him with amused astonishment. "It seems," she said finally, "that baby is growing."

III

THE next morning they went through the little court at the back of the hotel, and following the lane, they crossed the bridge and came to the Piazza. When it burst upon them he stood speechless, but she clapped her hands and cried, "See the chairs before the cafés, and the waiters in their white aprons. There is a woman with a Virot hat. I had one like it last year. She has put it on wrong — she is English."

"But the church!" said Angelo. "Brother Ambrose told me once that, of all the works of man's hands, this is the most beautiful."

She glanced at the east end of the Piazza and shrugged her shoulders. "Another church," she said. "That will wait for a rainy day when we cannot sit in front of the cafés and eat ices, and feed the pigeons and listen to the band. You may take your time with churches; they will not run away."

But at eleven o'clock there fluttered up the three flagstaffs in front of St. Mark's the banner of Italy, and the loungers about Florian's café started in groups toward the cathedral.

"Come," said Dolores, "we may as well see your church to-day. It seems to be fashionable."

As they crossed the Piazza her eyes caught the four gilded horses from the Arch of Nero. "I like those," she said; "they are alive."

They entered through the middle door, adorned with enamelled figures of the saints, and came at once into the glory of the place. Before them, up to the very altar steps, was a kneeling throng of people. Around them rose the walls of glass mosaics, of alabaster, of precious marbles and hammered gold. From the domes the light filtered through the smoke of the censers ; and far away, above the high altar, glowed the Pala d'Oro.

A priest held up the Host, and out of the silence came the far-off note of a silver bell. Angelo fell upon his knees. Again the sweet sound throbbed through the air.

Dolores bent over him, and he felt a tear upon his hand. "Take me away," she sobbed. "Quick, or I shall be praying."

They went out onto the Piazza and walked slowly through the arcade on the right. They did not speak. At the photographer's, near the corner, Dolores stopped and looked at the pictures in the window.

"There is Calvé," she said, "and Bernhardt, and Monsieur Gladstone. He should change his valet." Then she gave a cry and ran into the shop. Angelo followed her.

"No, no," she was saying to the attendant; "not that one—that is Jean de Reszke—the one in the corner," and she leaned over and pointed eagerly.

The shopman handed her a picture.

She seized it, looked at it, and then pressed it to her bosom.

"Look," she cried, half laughing, half crying, "it is Juan. Isn't he grand? See; he is wearing the scarf I gave to him. Look at his silk stockings—how white they are."

She held the picture away from her and made a courtesy.

"Very fine we are to-day, Monsieur Juan," she said. "What woman tied your jabot for you?"

She asked the price of the picture.

"A lira, Signora."

"Too little," she said, and she put a gold piece on the counter.

That evening she was very quiet. About nine o'clock she rang for the waiter and asked him to bring writing materials. She did not write easily, and she was obliged to ask Angelo the spelling of one or two simple words. When she finally sealed and addressed her letter he offered to post it for her.

"It is of no consequence," she said.

"It is to my dressmaker. I must be getting ready for the autumn." Presently, she went out and posted it herself.

They spent the next two days upon the water. They floated from the Piazza through the Grand Canal, under the iron bridge, to the Canal de Mestre, by the side of which lies the Ghetto. They glided over the tideless lagoons to Murano; they skirted the shores of Saint Lazzaro, where the white-walled monastery stands among the trees, and, best of all, they took a "barca," and the two rowers drove them out against the warm wind to the Lido.

The third day she said to him, "I have a headache. The sun on the water has been too much for me. I shall sleep until the evening; then I shall be well again. You must spend the day by yourself. It will be the first. Go out to the Lido again and tell me all about it when you return."

He demurred, but she said, "If you stay here you will be coming in every half-hour to ask if I am better, and I shall not sleep." So he submitted.

She called him back as he reached the door. "Do not dare to look at any of the women on the beach. If you do I shall know it. I have only to look into your eyes."

He had his hand upon the latch when she called again, "Angelo." He came back eagerly.

"You are sure that you do not regret?"

He shook his head. "I only regret the years before you came," he said.

She looked at him for a moment, then she put out her arms, drew him toward her, and kissed him on the forehead.

"Good-by," she said. "Do not come back if I call again."

He went out. As he was going down the stairs he heard her call his name, and stopped, then he remembered her injunction, and went on. If he had disobeyed, who knows?

He went to the Lido, but the light had gone out of the sky, the breeze from the Adriatic was cold, the band played out of tune, and his luncheon choked him. He walked up and down the sands, waiting until he might go back to Venice, where there was sunlight, where the breeze was warm, where, in the Piazza, the band played sweetly and the pigeons perched and cooed on the carved statues of the saints. At three o'clock he started to walk to the quay—the tram-cars were too slow. He found his barca just off the landing steps, and he bade the men row fast.

"I am very late," he said.

He flung himself upon the cushions and shut his eyes.

"Pietro," he said to the man at the after oar, "were you ever in love?"

"A thousand times, signore," replied Pietro, showing his white teeth.

"Is she waiting for you?" asked Angelo.

"I fear she is, signore."

"Row faster, then," said Angelo; and rising, he flung his weight upon the oar.

They landed at the Piazza, and it was only four o'clock. He did not dare to go home.

"She said she should sleep until evening," he thought. "If I go home now I shall disturb her."

He wandered about the Piazza looking at the shop windows. He passed the glass-makers, the jewellers, and the print-shop. He crossed to the other side and walked slowly by the cafés and the booksellers. Then he came to the little flower-shop. In the window were some yellow mimosa blossoms. He went in and bought them. It was now half-past four. He would go to the hotel, but not up-stairs. Perhaps the concierge could tell him how Dolores was; perhaps he might see Nanette, her maid.

He went out of the Piazza, across the bridge, and through the lane, walking as slowly as possible. He entered the court-yard of the hotel. The concierge stood in the doorway.

"Ah, signore," he exclaimed, "the signora barely caught the train. She bade me give you this letter."

Angelo took it without a word, and

slowly opened it. It contained some Italian money and a scrap of paper on which
was written :

" Forget me.

" Dolores."

I

HE opened his eyes and saw a woman's face framed in white linen.

"If the geraniums flower too soon," he said feebly, "you must pinch off the blossoms with your fingers and—"

"Hush," said a sweet, low voice; and he closed his eyes and slept again.

The house surgeon made his rounds at ten o'clock. "How is your patient?" he asked of the Sister of Mercy who sat at the foot of Angelo's bed.

"Better," she replied. "He spoke just now of flowers. They all seem to speak of flowers or women when they are convalescent."

"Flowers and women are the same thing," said the surgeon with a bow, and he went up to the cot.

"Count d'Apremont?" he said. Angelo opened his eyes. "How are you this morning?"

[45]

"Very well," said Angelo, "but the geraniums—"

"He will do," said the surgeon to the nurse. "Plenty of nourishment and the same medicines."

A week afterward they let him sit on the balcony overlooking the Campo San Polo. Sister Frances sat by him.

"How far is it to Paris?" he asked.

"I do not know," she replied, "but it is the chief city of France, and to go to France one must turn to the right. I know that, for last summer the senior surgeon went to France, and I saw him go out of the door and turn to the right. I do not know much about such things. I am religious."

"Did you ever know a man named Juan?" he asked, after a pause.

"Juan? Juan?" she said, reflecting. "Oh, yes, the old Spanish gardener at the convent in Turin was called Juan. He gave me some flowers the day I came away to begin my nursing."

"The Juan that I mean was not a gardener," said Angelo. "He was a man with broad shoulders and a thick neck. He had black hair and a smooth face, except that he had whiskers just to the bottom of his ears. He wore a velvet jacket with many buttons, and long, white silk stockings. He had a scarf about his waist and a lace jabot at his throat. He was a bull-fighter."

"I know no bull-fighters," said Sister Frances.

"If a man were to cut your arm with his knife because you spilled his tobacco," he asked presently, "would you love him for it?"

"It is time for your medicine," said Sister Frances.

At the end of another week the surgeon pronounced him cured.

"He is as well as he is likely to be," he said to the nurse, and he tapped his forehead with his fingers and shrugged his shoulders.

Angelo made a bundle of his monk's robe and sandals, which he tied up in a

large silk handkerchief. Everything else
he told Sister Frances she might give
away. Of the money which Dolores had
enclosed in her letter he kept a note for
fifty liras; the rest he gave to Sister
Frances. "For your poor," he said.

"I shall have no more poor," she exclaimed. "They will all be rich;" and
she turned away to hide her tears.

Then he shook hands with her and with
the surgeon, went down-stairs, through
the front door, and turned to the right.
As he passed the little balcony he looked
up and saw Sister Frances. She turned her
head away quickly and put her hands to
her eyes. When he reached the turning
in the narrow street he looked back. She
was still upon the balcony, and she put
out her arms toward him. He took off
his hat and then turned the corner.

"Signore," he said to the first man he
met, "will you kindly tell me the road
to France?"

The stranger looked at him, laughed,
and then walked away.

Angelo went on. Presently he crossed the canal by the iron bridge, and in a few moments he reached the railway station.

"Signore," he asked of a man in uniform, "is this the road to France?"

"Yes, signore," replied the official; "a train leaves for Turin and Paris in twenty minutes."

"Thank you," said Angelo, "but I shall walk," and crossing the long trestle which spans the lagoon, he began his journey.

II

IT was the evening of the last Sunday in September, and the boulevards were thronged. The hotels were full of Americans, and the favorite had won at Longchamps. The bourgeoisie was content.

At the restaurant César, on the Boulevard Poissonière, they dine early. At half-past four Henri, the head waiter, shaved and changed his collar. At five, Madame César, her gray hair arranged in puffs, put on her lace cap with the pink ribbons and took her seat behind the little

counter. At her left hand was a glass filled
with mignonette; at her right stood the
nickel vase into which the waiters cast the
pourboires, to be divided later. At a quarter
past five César himself came down-stairs
and arranged, on the table in the centre,
the grapes, the peaches, the melons, and
the green almonds. He stepped back and
regarded the effect—the mirrors, framed
in ebony and tarnished gold; the red velvet seats, somewhat worn; the linen on
the tables, white, but coarse; the shining
glasses; the fruits on the centre-table, and
his wife, with the pink ribbons, at the end
of the room.

"Good," he said, "but we need yellow," and he cut a great melon in halves
and laid them in a bed of green leaves.

At a quarter to six Monsieur Martin,
the engineer, entered. Madame Martin
followed him. His white, pointed beard
was closely trimmed, and he wore a red
ribbon in his button-hole. She was faded
and dressed in black. They took the table
in the corner, at the left of the door.

[50]

" *Bon jour, madame; bon jour, monsieur,*"
said Madame César. They read the menu
carefully, then monsieur said, in a loud and
confident voice, " *Sole frite et rump steak.*"

" As usual," whispered César to Henri,
and the fish was served almost instantly.

The door opened slowly and Angelo
came in. He carried a bundle in a silk
handkerchief and his clothes were worn
and travel-stained. He took off his hat
and bowed to Madame behind the counter, to the Martins, and to César.

"If it is not too dear," he said to the
latter, "I should like some soup and a
piece of bread."

"It will be one franc, monsieur."

Angelo hesitated. Then Madame César coughed and said, "Monsieur, soup
and bread cost fifty centimes ; a franc in-
cludes butter."

Angelo seated himself and put his
bundle under his chair.

"Be pleased to omit the butter," he said.

Henri served him with *petite marmite*
and a long loaf of bread.

"Did you ever see such eyes?" whispered Madame César to her husband. "I wonder what he has in his bundle?"

"Silverware," said César.

"You are stupid," she replied. "No thief ever had such eyes."

"A few more pairs like them would ruin us," said her husband. "You cut the price in two. If a blind man comes in perhaps you will double it."

"Go speak to him," said madame. "Find out something about him. It is easy to see that he is a gentleman and that he is ill."

By this time many of the tables were occupied. César made the rounds; a bow to one, a joke with another, a slight service to a third. At length he came to Angelo, who had emptied the tureen and was now eating the last of the bread.

"Will not monsieur have a little more of the soup?" asked César.

"I should like it," replied Angelo, "but I have very little money."

"When one orders soup," said César,

"he is entitled to all that he wishes. It is the rule of the house."

"In that case," said Angelo, "I will have some more; and bread, also, if it is permitted."

"Monsieur is a traveller?" ventured César.

"Yes," replied Angelo. "I came from Venice this evening."

"From Venice? Then you arrived by the express at five o'clock, at the Gare de Lyon?"

"No," replied Angelo; "I walked."

"Yes, from the station?"

"No, from Venice."

"Monsieur!" exclaimed César, "that is more than six hundred miles."

"Yes," said Angelo, "but I left Venice the last day of July. I came to see a woman—"

"Monsieur," said César, "many young men come to Paris for that purpose."

"Her name is Dolores," continued Angelo. "Do you know where I can find her?"

[53]

"She must be Spanish," said César. "Is she an artiste, a singer, an actress?"

"She is a dancer," replied Angelo.

"I do not think she comes here," said César. "Most of my patrons are serious. There is Monsieur Martin, the celebrated engineer, at the table in the corner. Madame is with him. They have dined here for ten years at a quarter to six. They read the menu from *hors-d'œuvres* to cheese and then he orders fried sole and rump steak. We have those dishes ready for him at a quarter to six. On his last name-day he ordered *langouste* and *vol-au-vent à la financière*, but before Henri reached the door monsieur called him back. 'Henri,' he said, 'on second thought, I will have fried sole and rump steak.' He will know nothing of your dancer. His habits are formed.

"The lady at the next table," he continued, "the large lady with the blue hat and the slight moustache, might doubtless have helped us twenty years ago, when she led the ballet at the Grand Opéra,

[54]

but she has ceased to be of the world. She is a compatriot of mine. She comes from Marseilles. She dines here each Friday and Sunday. We serve *bouillabaisse* on Friday, and I always keep some over for Sunday. *Bouillabaisse* is much better, monsieur, at its second cooking."

He looked slowly about the room.

"If Monsieur Vallon were here—ah, there he is, in the far corner. He is of the press. He knows every one."

He went over and spoke to a small man who, between the courses of his dinner, was correcting proofs. They evidently had their joke together, for César came back smiling.

"Monsieur," he said, "it seems that your friend is famous. She dances at the Folies-Bergères. She has an apartment on the avenue Friedland. Each fine day she drives a bay cob and a morning cart in the Bois. She drinks two glasses of warm milk at the Pré Catelan, and lunches at the Madrid. Her appetite is good. In the afternoon she drives in a victoria or a brougham, according to the weather. Her servants are English. They wear dark green and no rosettes. They are correctly dressed and do not attempt to speak French. Her brougham horses were given her by an English milord. They are very taking, but the nigh one is unsound. After she has danced in the evening she has supper at Paillard's. She dances at half-past nine. Her maid is a Frenchwoman, named Nanette. On Tuesdays and Saturdays madame has a *masseuse* for an hour. On Fridays she confesses at the Madeleine. Her costumes for the stage are made in Madrid, those for the carriage and the house she procures from Raudnitz and Jeanne Hallée, and her morning gowns are sent to her from London. Hellstern makes her slippers and he tries them on four times. Next winter she dances in St. Petersburg, and in the spring she goes to America. At the Folies-Bergères she receives two thousand francs each night and half the gross receipts of each Sunday. She keeps an

[56]

account at the Crédit Lyonnais. Monsieur Vallon makes you his compliments and regrets that he cannot give you more definite information."

"And Juan?" asked Angelo. "Did he say nothing of a bull-fighter called Juan?"

César became interested in the salt-cellar.

"Did he speak of Juan?" Angelo asked again.

César blushed and drummed upon the table with his fingers. Then he leaned over and whispered, "Monsieur Vallon's advice is that you return to Venice."

III

ANGELO paid for his dinner and gave Henri two sous as a *pourboire*. Then, with his bundle in his hand, he bowed to Madame César.

"Good night, monsieur," she said, and she followed him with her eyes to the door.

César gave him his route.

"The first turn to the right, monsieur, then the third street is the rue Richer.

Turn to the right again and you will come
to the Folies-Bergères."

The rue Richer was crowded with
cabs. Their lamps made two lines of
lights so long that they narrowed in the
distance. Over the door of the theatre,
traced in gas-jets, blazed the word "Dolores."

Angelo entered the vestibule. Two
men in evening dress sat within the rail-
ing of the bureau, and a member of the
municipal police stood by the green door
at the left, his helmet, breastplate, and
jack-boots glittering in the gas-light.

"Your ticket, if you please, monsieur,"
said the cashier.

"I have come to see Dolores," said
Angelo.

"Doubtless," rejoined the cashier,
"but have you a place? You are just in
time."

"No," replied Angelo, "I have no
place. I do not understand these matters
very well, monsieur. I have not been of
the world long. I arrived in Paris only

[58]

this evening. I came from Venice, monsieur. Before that I was in Rome. The
marionettes in Rome are very fine, monsieur. They walk and dance, and the tall
one in the blue jacket smokes a cigarette.
Dolores said that they were much more
amusing than the Coliseum, but that, I
believe, is very fine also. In Venice I was
quite ill, monsieur. Dolores left me there.
She was obliged to come to Paris to see
her dressmaker and—"

"Excuse me, monsieur," said the cashier, "but if you have no ticket you are
too late. All the places are taken. You
may stand in the upper balcony, but it
is very crowded. The admission is two
francs."

Angelo put his hand in his pocket.

"Monsieur," he said, after counting
his money, "I have but one franc and
eighty centimes."

"Take it and get rid of him," whispered the assistant, who was adding up
the night's receipts; and the cashier
handed Angelo a ticket.

He went up-stairs, crossed the glass-roofed garden where the palm trees are, then up another flight, and came to the second balcony.

It was crowded with workmen in their Sunday clothes, with men from the clubs, with women from the streets. The heat was intense and the foul air reeked with the scent of patchouly. The slope of the balcony was very abrupt, and thanks to his height, Angelo could see the stage and the two *loges* next to the proscenium arch. The drop-curtain was down and the sign " *Entre-acte* " was posted.

"Where is Dolores?" asked Angelo.

A girl who stood next to him looked at his bundle, laughed, and said, "She's having a bottle with Juan in her dressing-room." Then she looked in his face and said, "Pardon, monsieur, I thought you were one of us, but I see that I was stupid."

She was silent a moment and then she spoke again: "You may stand in front of me if you wish. I have seen her twice already. I come because the men come. She has the trick. She is no better looking than some of us, and the way in which she wears her hair, with little hooks over her ears, is very bad, but she is the mode, and then one has said it. The mode is a strange thing, monsieur. It depends upon trifles. Liane, who lives with me, went without her dinner for a month and then bought a hat in the rue de la Paix. She is down there in the stalls with a head clerk from the Bon Marché, and I am up here in the second balcony. But," she said with a laugh, "I had the thirty dinners, and they are better than a head clerk."

"You perceive, monsieur," she added, "that with such principles I shall never be the mode."

"Are you cold?" she asked suddenly. "You are shivering."

"No," he replied. "But Dolores,—is she not coming?"

Just then the prompter gave the three spats and the members of the orchestra came from under the stage and took their seats. Angelo could see a man with a blond beard enter the *loge* on the left. Presently a man seated himself in the *loge* on the right. He wore a dinner-jacket, a folded collar, cut very low in front, and a red cravat. He was dark, with closely cut hair, and he was continually rolling cigarettes which he lighted and then threw away.

"Look," said Angelo's neighbor; "there they are, the English milord and Juan. They say milord has castles and yachts and jewels and all such things, and poor old Juan has nothing but his smile and his courage and his cigarettes, and Dolores sides with Juan. That is eccentric, and it makes her *à la mode*."

The leader tapped with his baton and the music began; a picked string here, a tap of the kettle-drums there, a bleat from the oboe, a twinkle from the clarionets, a blare from the trombones, a wave of the white gloves, a burst of concerted sound, and the curtain went slowly up.

[62]

The stage was a blank. The orchestra glided into the "Spanish Dances," and from the wings stepped Dolores.

She was dressed in black. Her bodice, her skirts, her stockings, all were black. So small and perfectly shaped were her feet that she had the audacity to wear white slippers; and over her left ear rested the stem of a crimson rose.

She walked slowly down the stage, demure, her eyes cast down. She came into the glow of the foot-lights, stopped, and cast a glance toward the box on the right. Then she went half-way up the stage again, and the orchestra burst into full melody.

She stood motionless a moment, and then her body began to sway. The time was so exquisitely marked that the audience found itself swaying in unison. There was a tap of the kettle-drums, a change of rhythm, and she came whirling down the stage, a cloud of black tulle and a suggestion of white linen. The music ended with a crash and she stopped

suddenly, her arms extended, her bosom
heaving. For a moment the audience
was as silent as the throng at St. Peter's
when the Host is elevated, or as they
who, hat in hand, file past the Sistine
Madonna. Then a man in the third row
stood up and waved his hat. Immediately
the house rose, men and women. They
clapped their hands, they shouted, they
flung flowers, cigarettes, hats, gloves,
coins upon the stage; and she, her cheeks
burning, her eyes glowing, took the red
rose from her hair, put it to her lips, and
then flung it into the *loge* on the right.
Juan caught it, and the curtain fell.

"You are not going?" said the girl to
Angelo. "She dances in a moment. That
was merely her appearance."

He looked at her with a smile so sad
that she felt the tears coming to her eyes
and marvelled at herself.

"Yes," he said. "I am going. I have
seen her once more. Why should I stay?
I thank you, mademoiselle, for your kind-
ness. Good night."

He made his way slowly through the crowd to the stairs. She followed him with her eyes and suddenly pushed after him and touched his shoulder.

"Where are you going?" she asked.

"I do not know," he answered.

She hesitated, and then said, "You have money?"

"I have nothing," he replied.

"Good!" she exclaimed; "I am rich, if I am not the mode. I have forty francs. I can afford to be respectable for a week. Come."

She put her arm through his, and half supporting him, she led him out into the streets.

THE long, hot summer passed slowly at La Trappe; and when winter came it found the monastery unchanged, save that the graves of the monks had grown a little deeper and the Abbot had grown much older. All during the year he had worked with the feverish energy of a man who has a task to accomplish and finds his time short. His candle burned late every night, and with the strange freemasonry that prevails in all communities condemned to silence, the monks asked one another, "What has befallen the Abbot?"

One night in December the rain which had been steadily falling turned to snow, and in the morning, when the chapter went to the chapel at seven o'clock for "prime," the terrace by the fountain was covered with feathery flakes an inch deep. Such a thing had not been seen in Algeria for years. As the long file of brown-robed monks passed through the courtyard, one of them, a black-bearded Belgian, broke from the line, and flinging himself down rolled in the snow.

"My God," he cried, "see the snow, the snow that falls in Brussels. I made a statue of it in the park and won a prize. Marie came to see it. She said—"

Brother Ambrose whispered in his ear, and he rose and sullenly resumed his place in the line.

When Brother Ambrose reported this occurrence to the Abbot it was with fear and trembling. He remembered that Angelo had spoken in reply to a woman and had disappeared, "to work his penance," as the Abbot had said the next day. But Brother Pierre's offence had been gratuitous; no one had spoken to him, and the whole household had heard him utter a woman's name. It was not merely an offence, it was a scandal.

The Abbot listened calmly to the report, and then went to his desk and took out of it the red book with the lock.

[67]

"Marie was the name he spoke, was it not?" he asked.

"Yes, father," replied Brother Ambrose.

The Abbot opened the book, turned several leaves, ran his finger down a page, paused, and then locked the book and put it back in the desk.

"My friend," he said finally, "I fear that more men turn monks for the love of a woman than for the love of God."

Brother Ambrose drew his hand across his eyes and stood silent.

The Abbot paced the little room, his hands behind his back.

"Yes," he continued, "who resuscitated our order? Armand de Rance. He was a brave man who stood well with his king. He loved the Duchess Rohan-Montbazon, and she loved him. One day the king sent him into Germany on a mission. The duchess begged him not to leave her; but he said, 'The king wills it, and my honor compels me.' And she said, 'Thy honor is my honor,' and kissed

[68]

him, and he rode away. When in a month
he returned to Paris, successful in his mission, he rode gayly to her house, and getting off his horse, ran past the domestics,
up the stairs to her room, and found her
there, dead, upon a bier, the candles burning. Had she lived, there would have been
no La Trappe. You took the vows, my
friend, because forty years ago a little
flaxen-haired girl in Normandy played
you false. Shall I tell you her name? It
is all in the red book, yonder."

"No," cried brother Ambrose, "do
not speak it. I hear it in my dreams; I
hear it continually by day—in the prayers—in the chants—in the gospel and
epistle—in every breeze that blows. Do
not speak it."

"Forgive me," said the Abbot. "I
hoped that forty years had brought you
peace."

There was a long silence, and then the
Abbot spoke again.

"You remember," he said, "when I
came to La Trappe, do you not?"

[69]

"Yes," replied Brother Ambrose, "I let you in at the gate. You rode a black horse and wore an officer's uniform. You carried Angelo, who was a baby then, in your arms. You gave him to me, and I brought him up on goat's milk. You told me that he was the son of an officer who had died in the desert."

"I lied to you," said the Abbot.

"I thought so at the time," said Brother Ambrose.

"I wrote the same lie in the red book," added the Abbot.

Brother Ambrose shook his head gravely.

"What is more," said the Abbot, "on the day that Angelo helped you in the guest-room, I read the lie to him."

"You disowned him?" gasped Brother Ambrose.

"Yes, God help me," said the Abbot, "I disowned my son."

"You perceive," he added, "what manner of man your Abbot is."

"I presume," suggested Brother Ambrose, faintly, "you thought it for the best?"

"Yes," said the Abbot, bitterly, "I have tried that salve, but it does not heal. A lie is never for the best. What right had I, because the world had gone wrong with me, to teach my son that the grave is the only happiness that comes to man? What right had I to tell him he was fatherless and had nothing to link him with the world? My grief made me self-ish. I forgot all the joys of living; I saw only the face of a girl lying dead in the little house in Biskra. I often see it, and I often hear her sweet voice asking, 'Where is my son, for whom I died?' And the only answer I can make is, 'I disowned him and he went away.' God came to me in the garden the last night that Angelo was here, and I went to the chapel cell to make confession; but I was too late; the lock was broken and my son was a wanderer. He had no money, no knowledge of the world, no friends. That was almost a year ago, and I have heard no word of him. Is he ill, is he homeless, is he famishing, or is he with his mother in heaven? If so, what must they two think of the Holy Abbot of La Trappe? What do you think of him? You came to me to-night to ask me to fix a penance for Brother Pierre. His offence is that he spoke the name of the woman who loved him years ago. He simply spoke aloud what you and I whisper every hour of the day. It is true the monastery has its rules, but who am I that I should enforce them? I can only say, God bless him."

"Amen," said Brother Ambrose.

"To-morrow," resumed the Abbot, "is Christmas Day. I wish the discipline to be somewhat relaxed. Serve out fresh straw for the chapter and let them sit in the refectory for a half-hour after dinner. You will be celebrant at the high mass."

"I!" exclaimed Brother Ambrose, "Why not you?"

"Because," said the Abbot, "I shall not be here. This is my last day at La Trappe."

Brother Ambrose staggered back against the wall.

The Abbot took from his desk a letter. "I have written fully to the Superior," he said, "and I wish that you would post this after I am gone. The accounts of the chapter are made up to this morning. We have had a very good year. Here are my keys," and he held them out to Brother Ambrose, who stood motionless.

The Abbot looked at him a moment, and then placed the keys upon the desk.

"I have ordered a carriage from Algiers to be at the gate at eleven o'clock," he continued. "I shall go out as I am, but in the guest-room I shall leave my robe and shall put on ordinary dress, which will be brought me in the carriage. I wish that you would keep my rosary and crucifix, as a remembrance. I shall remain in Algiers only long enough to make some inquiries, and shall then go wherever it seems best. If it should be necessary to communicate with me, the Superior has an address. By the way, do

you know my name? I am Count Charles
François d'Apremont. A good name till
I soiled it."

Just then the great bell at the gate
clanged.

The Abbot started. "The carriage!"
he exclaimed. "I thought it was earlier.
Go and see."

"No, no," cried Brother Ambrose,
starting from the wall and placing himself against the door. "You must not go.
You shall not go."

"Silence," said the Abbot, sternly.
"Remember that until I have passed
the gate I am the Abbot of La Trappe.
Afterwards," he added gently, "I shall be
nothing but an old man seeking his son."

Brother Ambrose bowed his head and
went slowly out.

The Abbot arranged the books and
papers in his desk with great care, then
he turned the key and left it in the lock.
He glanced about the little room he was
so soon to leave. Its whitewashed walls
and stone floor were dimly lighted by

the candle. Its sole furnishings were the
desk, a single chair, the coffin bed in the
corner, and near the door a bench, upon
which was a basin and a water-pitcher of
red clay. It was all hideously clean and
bare, but still it had been a home. The
Abbot marvelled at the reluctance with
which he quitted it.

The door opened slowly, and Brother
Ambrose whispered, "It was the carriage. I bade the coachman wait a little
distance down the road."

"Good," said the Abbot. "I am ready."

At the door he turned and waved his
hand.

"Adieu, little chamber," he said, and
then he went out, leaving the candle
burning.

The two old men went slowly through
the courtyard. The rain had ceased, and
the sky was filled with broken clouds
swept toward the Great Desert by the
wind.

At the gate the Abbot stopped and
fumbled at his girdle.

"Here," he said, "take this before I go out," and he thrust his rosary into Brother Ambrose's hand.

"Now open the gate."

Just then a faint noise came from the dark shadow of the eucalyptus trees. Some one was coming. They could hear him splashing through the pools of water that lay upon the rain-drenched road. The moon shone out from between the edges of the clouds, and the Abbot saw the figure of a man approaching. It came on slowly, and the Abbot and Brother Ambrose stepped behind the great stone gate-post. The footsteps came close up to the gate, then stopped; a pale, drawn face was thrust between the bars and a faint voice whispered, "Open."

The Abbot turned white and fell to trembling. He did not speak while Brother Ambrose was busy with the lock. But when, a moment later, he flung his arms about his son, Brother Ambrose heard him whisper the one word, "Miriam."

Angelo did not notice it, nor did he seem to see the two old men. He breathed sobbingly, as if he had been running.

"Quick!" he gasped, throwing himself against the gate, "shut it and keep it out!"

"What?" asked Brother Ambrose.

"The world," said Angelo; "it is pursuing me."

They shut the gate and locked it.

Angelo gazed about him as if in a dream. He had resumed his monk's robe, and it was wet and splashed with mire to the waist. He was so tired and weak that he swayed as he stood.

"The geraniums;" he said finally, and he started toward the garden.

The Abbot put his arm about his son's waist, and they crossed the courtyard and went down the grass walk together. When they came to the geraniums they found nothing but long rows of brown stalks, cut back for the winter. In the trenches between the rows the water lay in sullen pools. Angelo stood silent for a time, and then he said, "It must be winter. What has become of the summer?"

"It has gone," replied the Abbot, sadly, "but," he added, "it will come again."

They went slowly up the grass walk, neither of them speaking.

As they reached the Abbot's chamber the moon shone out full and clear. The Abbot paused on the threshold.

"Look, my son," he said, and he pointed to the cross on the chapel roof. "For those who are weary and heavy-laden there alone is peace."

They entered the little chamber, and the Abbot closed the door.

Brother Ambrose, who had followed them afar off, took his seat on a bench in the cloisters, within call, and waited.

In half an hour the Abbot came out and called him softly.

He went up to the door.

"Hush," whispered the Abbot, "he is sleeping. Is the carriage still waiting?"

"Yes, Father," replied Brother Ambrose.

"Pay the coachman a double fare and send him away," said the Abbot.

"And the clothes in the carriage?" asked Brother Ambrose.

The Abbot hesitated. "You may give them to the coachman, also," he said finally.

"Thank God," said Brother Ambrose. "Shall I celebrate the mass to-morrow?"

"No," said the Abbot.

"Then you had better take this, Father," said Brother Ambrose, and he handed the Abbot his rosary.

"Good night," said the Abbot.

"Good night, Father," said Brother Ambrose.

The clock over the refectory door struck twelve.

It was Christmas morning.

TROT, TROT
TO MARKET

TROT, TROT
TO MARKET

I

WHEN the Earl of Vauxhall left the smoking-room of the Celibates Club (he had been divorced many years and was theoretically eligible), he was followed by laughter and clapping of hands. A man of three score and ten, he had told a story that may not be told here. There were French phrases scattered through it at which the men who did not know French laughed, and at which those who did shifted uneasily in their chairs and wondered why they were there. A few toothless skeletons in fur coats, who sat about the fire, cackled and winked and nudged each other and, dying, saluted him.

When the earl reached the lobby he spoke to the porter.

"Shaw," he asked, "is there a note for me?" and while Shaw was searching

among the post-boxes, the earl took oc-
casion to stagger, to clutch at his collar,
to collapse upon the porter's seat, and
thence to slide to the floor and lie still:
a heap of fur coat, top hat, white gloves,
patent leather, and dead clay.

"Yes, my lord," said Shaw, turning,
"here is —"

Colonel Mellish, who just then came
into the club, was the first to reach the
prostrate nobleman. The colonel had seen
many things and was not easily rattled.
He raised the peer's head and loosened
his cravat.

"Shaw," asked the colonel in a low
voice, "what is it, — apoplexy or the
booze?"

"I'm sure, sir, I can't say," gasped
Shaw. "It might be either, sir. His lordship has been here since luncheon waiting for a note which just came, sir."

"Have you it?" asked the colonel.

"Yes, sir," said Shaw, and he held out
a dainty white envelope.

"Better hold onto it," said the colonel,

[84]

"it is probably not from the Bishop of London."

Just then a man came into the lobby. The colonel looked up.

"Ah, Dr. Hardy," he said, "here is something in your line. I resign."

The doctor kneeled, pulled open the peer's coat, in the buttonhole of which was a white carnation, felt for the heart and the pulse, looked into the eyes, stood, and took off his hat.

"He is dead," he said.

"Quick work," said the colonel. "No chance for bets. I could have got two to one in the smoking-room that it was nothing but the booze."

He stood a moment, looking down at the heap on the marble floor.

"Doctor," he said at length, "what was it we used to have at school — something about *de mortuis?* There was more of it, but I forget it. Now, just between you and Shaw and me, I wish to say that that thing lying there was a peer of England three minutes ago, and that he didn't

[85]

have a friend. I 'll leave him to you. You have the smartest practice in the West End — and the largest death-rate."

He started toward the door, paused, and came back.

"Shaw," he whispered, "where 's that note ?"

"Here, sir," replied Shaw.

"Give it to me," said the colonel.

"But, sir," said Shaw, "the rules are very strict about members' letters."

"How is it addressed ?" asked the colonel.

"To the Earl of Vauxhall, sir," replied Shaw.

"Who *is* the Earl of Vauxhall ?" asked the colonel.

Shaw stared. "There he is, sir," he said finally, pointing to the floor.

"Nonsense," said the colonel, "that 's nobody. I 'm going to see the earl, and I 'll give him his letter."

"Oh," said Shaw, "you mean Lord Robert, sir? He *is* the earl now, sure enough, sir," and he handed over the note.

"Call a hansom," said the Colonel.

II

IT was only a moment's drive down Piccadilly and up Clarges Street, when the colonel held his stick to the left and the hansom stopped. The colonel sat so long that cabby opened the trap and asked, "Is this right, your honor?"

"Yes," replied the colonel. "I'm thinking; don't bother me. You're Irish, are you not?"

"Well, your honor," said cabby, "that depends."

"Upon what?" demanded the colonel.

"Upon what your honor is," replied cabby.

"Enough," said the colonel, "we are countrymen;" and he stepped to the sidewalk and handed up a shilling.

"Don't break your hand," said cabby.

"I won't," said the colonel, with a laugh. "Are you married?"

"I am, your honor," replied cabby.

"And one at the breast, I expect," said the colonel.

"Two, your honor," said cabby, grinning.

"Good," said the colonel; "we are a pair of rogues, but I have n't another shilling in the world."

"I 'll lend your honor four bob," said cabby, standing on the perch and going for his pocket.

"No, thanks," said the colonel. "I don't want another creditor, but I 'd shake your hand if I had n't just touched carrion."

"I 'm even with your honor," said cabby, "I 've just had a sandwich at the shelter."

They parted with mutual regret, and the colonel rang the bell of a little house with a green light over the door.

"Is Lord Robert at home ?" he asked.

"Yes, sir," said the servant, and the colonel went up the stairs, stumbled at the top step, swore, and knocked.

"Come," said some one, and the colonel entered.

[88]

"I'm a bit late," he said, "but the King is dead! long live the King."

A young man with hair the color of ripe wheat, with black eyebrows, with a waist like an hour-glass, with a skin like milk, and a voice like cream, said, "What are you rowing about? You've got a place to sleep, I suppose; why don't you go to it?"

"Faith," said the colonel, "that's a fine way to greet the bearer of glad tidings. I've a mind not to tell you, but I must, it's too good to keep; your father has been dead half an hour."

"What do you mean?" exclaimed the young man.

"Just what I say," replied the colonel. "Your respected parent had a stroke in the vestibule of the Celibates and never moved after it. You're bearin' up wonderfully, my lad. I know what a blow it is to you. You're an earl, and through no fault of your own. I trust, my lord, that if any patronage comes your way you won't forget that Colonel Mellish

spent his last shilling to bring you this
news. You might give me a drink now.
I've a bad taste in my mouth."

The Earl of Vauxhall motioned toward
a corner of the room, and the colonel went
to a cabinet, opened it, and took out a
decanter, a glass, and a syphon. He mixed
a drink, drank it, mixed another, and came
back, with the glass in his hand. He took
a seat by the fire and watched the earl
pace the floor.

"Bobby," asked the colonel, after a sip
or two, "how long is it since you and the
lamented had speech together?"

"Rather more than five years," replied
the earl. "Did he speak of me to-night?"

"He didn't speak at all," said the
colonel. "He just wheezed a bit and was
off. He'd been drinking well all day, Shaw
told me, so we've every reason to suppose
he died happy. Oh, he was a fine old
English gentleman!"

"If you think," said the earl, "that you
gratify me by these remarks, you are mis-
taken. While he was alive, it was one

[90]

thing. Now that he is dead, it is quite another. You will oblige me by either being decent or going."

The colonel laughed. "All right, my lord," he said. "I came to talk a little business. You owe me a thousand pounds. I suppose it will soon be convenient to pay, now that you have come into the property."

"Property!" laughed the earl, "there isn't any. The land is mortgaged up to its neck. The town house went years ago, and the pictures and the bric-a-brac were sold in '96. My father leaves me nothing but his title and his reputation. As for me, I have three hundred a year from my mother, in a trust; I sell a little wine to my friends; I occasionally help an artist to get rid of a picture; now and then I get a tip on the horses, and I have been known to play cards—witness my debt to you. I owe more money than I ever had."

The colonel sat gazing into the fire.

"Bobby," he said at length, "it looks

as though you would have to sell something."

"I 've got a Waterbury watch," said the earl.

"I brought you something to-night that is rather valuable," said the colonel.

"What is it?" asked the young man.

"An earldom," replied the colonel, "and there 's a rich American born every minute."

The young man laughed again. "Do you know a possible purchaser?" he asked.

"I do," replied the colonel. "There 's one just around the corner in Park Lane. She is the daughter of a man who lived in Montana or Delaware or some other Western place. He salted mines and then sold them. He built railroads and then wrecked them. He went to Congress and worked the stock market. He died six months ago and left his daughter a matter of sixty thousand a year. My cousin, Matt Cassidy, was the old man's private secretary, and he sent me all the particulars when the girl came over. She 's here with her aunt, the only relation she has. They brought letters to the Embassy, but they don't know many people yet, being in mourning for the old pirate. They do things in style. They have as good horses as go in London, and a better cook than there is in Buckingham Palace."

"Have you seen her?" asked the earl.

"Faith, I have, and twice," replied the colonel. "Both times in the Park, and Bobby, my boy, she's the sweetest thing that ever came out of the States."

"How old is she?" asked the earl, with some animation.

"Just one and twenty," replied the colonel. "She got her money in February. I have a list of her securities that Matt sent me. At present prices she's worth over a million."

"Pounds?" asked the earl.

"Of course," said the colonel.

"You seem to have been thorough," said the earl.

"In my business," said the colonel, "you've got to be thorough."

[93]

"What is her name?" asked the earl.

The colonel went to the corner and mixed himself another drink. "Bobby," he said, "before I tell you that, we ought to have an understanding. I don't want much."

"What are your terms?" asked the earl.

"Cash is one thing," said the colonel, "and a contingent fee is another."

"That's reasonable," said the earl.

"I must have the thousand you owe me, and nine more to go with it," said the colonel.

"You shall have it," said the earl.

"And in addition," continued the colonel, "I want the run of the house. I want to be the friend of the family, with a seat in the chimney-corner. I'm getting old, and I'm looking into the question of reform."

"Agreed," said the earl, laughing.

"Shake," said the colonel, and they joined hands.

"Now," said the colonel, glancing about the room and lowering his voice,

"I'll tell you her name. It's Harwood. Catherine Harwood. Don't forget it."

"I sha'n't," said the earl; "but how am I to meet her?"

"Leave that to me," replied the colonel. "Good night."

He rose unsteadily, took his overcoat from the sofa, and struggled into it. He buttoned it slowly and put his hands into the pockets for his gloves.

"Hello," he said, "I was near forgetting. The late earl, of blessed memory, was waiting all day at the club for this note. It came just too late to catch him. He had been so anxious about it that I thought it might be important, so I brought it along. You'd best open it."

The earl took the letter and broke the seal. He read the contents under the lamp.

"It seems," he said, "that my dear old father got ahead of us."

"What is it?" asked the colonel.

The earl read aloud:

"*Dear Lord Vauxhall,—I have thought it*
"*all over by myself, and I have talked it all*

[95]

"*over with my aunt, and my answer is —*
"*yes.*
"*I shall be at home all to-morrow afternoon,*
"*and shall look for you at any hour.*
Very sincerely,
Catherine Harwood.
"*Wednesday.*"

"What!" shouted Colonel Mellish.

The earl tossed the note across the table.

"No," said the colonel. "You read it again. I haven't got my glasses."

The earl complied. When he had finished, the colonel went slowly to the corner and took the decanter in his trembling hand. The bottle clicked against the glass as he poured.

"Here's to the late Earl of Vauxhall," he said. "He was a past-master. Old, hideous, bankrupt, disgraced, he knew how to make the richest girl in London say —yes. Our cake is dough, but I drink to him."

"It occurs to me," said the earl, "that you have had drink enough. Your mind seems a bit flabby."

"How so?" asked the colonel.

"She did n't marry him, did she?" asked the earl.

"No," replied the colonel.

"But she said she *would*, did n't she?" The colonel nodded.

"He 's dead, is n't he?"

"Dead?" exclaimed the colonel, with a shudder. "If you had seen him on the floor—"

"Well, then," continued the earl, "is it vanity that suggests that, if she were willing to marry the late earl, she may be willing to marry the present one?"

The colonel staggered to his feet, and threw his arms about his companion's neck.

"Damn it," he cried, "we 'll have her yet. The old man did all the work and the young one gets the girl—"

"Sit down," said the earl, pushing him off. "Don't put your hands on me, man. You 're drunk."

Colonel Mellish fell into his chair.

"You 'll go now," continued the earl.

[97]

"I shall step around to my father's rooms. I don't suppose they will let me in, but I'll give them a chance. Come — good night."

The colonel reached the door with effort. "When will you see the girl?" he asked.

"To-morrow," replied the earl. "I sha'n't need to be presented. I'll go by myself. What's the number of the house?"

"I've forgotten," said the colonel, "but it's the one with the conservatory in front. You can't miss it."

III

THE swift bolt of the gods had stricken the old Earl of Vauxhall so very late at night that the morning newspapers made no mention of the calamity. The new earl satisfied himself of this while at breakfast. He had come from his chamber dressed in black, and his first act was to send out his hat to be fitted with a deep band. The mirror told him that his mourning was becoming, and he ate his egg and drank his tea with more than usual satisfaction.

"I'm an earl at twenty-five, and there's sixty thousand a year waiting for me round the corner," he said to himself. "It might be worse."

He had been at his father's rooms the night before, and when he had finished his breakfast and the racing news in the papers, he took a cab again for Half Moon Street. His father's man let him in.

"Good morning, Dobbins," said the earl, "is everything right?"

"Yes, my lord," replied Dobbins, "I've just got him shaved and touched up a bit, and he looks very well, considering what he's been through. Will you go in, my lord?"

The earl hesitated. "No," he said, at length, "I don't think he would like it if he knew I were looking at him."

"I dare say not, my lord," ventured Dobbins. "He was a bitter hater."

"Has he never spoken of me in all these years?" asked the earl.

"Not in a way I ought to mention, my lord," replied Dobbins.

"I am sorry," said the earl, "but I had to stand by my mother."

"Yes, my lord," said Dobbins, "you did quite right, if I may be so bold."

"Thank you, Dobbins," said the earl. "You know more about it than any one else. By the way, there is no one that should be notified of the funeral, is there? I have wired my father's cousin, Mr. Whitstable. He is the only relative that I know of."

Dobbins shook his head. "I'm afraid, my lord," he said, "that the funeral will look like a creditors' meeting."

"Do you know a lady named Harwood?" asked the earl. "Miss Catherine Harwood?"

"No, my lord," said Dobbins, reflecting. "I don't recall the name. But then," he added, looking toward the chamber door, "he had so many."

"I suppose so," said the earl. "I will come in again this evening."

At his rooms he found Colonel Mellish awaiting him.

"Bobby, my lad," said the latter, "I dropped in to cheer you up a bit."

"And yourself, incidentally, I see," said the earl, pointing to the decanter on the table.

"I'm doing my best," replied the colonel, "but I'm in an awful funk. Suppose she won't have you?"

The earl caught a glimpse of himself in the mirror. "I think she'll have me fast enough," he said. "The only question is, has she got the money?"

"I have it in black and white," exclaimed the colonel.

"All right," said the earl. "We'll look over the schedules while we are eating our chop."

They lunched leisurely, and the schedules proved highly satisfactory.

"I don't know much about these American securities," said the earl, "but they certainly look well on paper."

"I've looked them all up," said the

colonel, "and they 're as good as the Bank."

The earl went into his chamber, added a few touches to his toilet, came back, and drew on a pair of black gloves.

"I 'm off," he said.

"God bless you," said the colonel. "You 'll find me here. Don't be long."

The earl took a visiting-card from his case, drew a pencil through the name, and wrote under the line, "The Earl of Vauxhall." Then he went out.

The house with the conservatory in front was not far down Park Lane, and the earl stopped his hansom before the door. He rang the bell, and a footman in powder took his card.

"Is Miss Harwood at home?" asked the earl.

"Yes, my lord," replied the man.

The earl went in, and was shown through the hall, past another footman, up the stairs, and into a small room on the left. He looked about him with approval.

"This will do, I think," he said to himself. "I'll make a few slight changes, but on the whole it will do. How those Americans spend money on flowers — bunches on the piano — on the mantel — on the cabinet — on the table ; four guineas, at least! I can save a bit there."

His ear caught the rustle of a skirt, and he turned quickly. A girl came into the room. She began speaking at the door.

"Ah, Lord Vauxhall," she said, "I was afraid you had repented." Then she stopped suddenly and gazed at the earl.

He bowed as if she were the queen.

"I am afraid there is some mistake," she said, smiling. "I expected to find the Earl of Vauxhall."

"Madam," said the young man, "I am the Earl of Vauxhall."

"There must be two of you, then," she said, laughing. "You certainly are not *my* Earl of Vauxhall."

"Madam," said the earl, "you doubtless expected to see my father. He died last night."

[103]

"Oh," she cried, "how terrible! How sorry I am for you."

"And I, for you," said the earl.

"For me?" she exclaimed.

"Yes," he said, with a smile that he made very sad, and a voice into which he put tears, "for you. My father and I have been estranged and have not spoken together in many years. Chance alone has made me acquainted with his great happiness—with his great loss."

The girl stood speechless, with wondering eyes.

"Just after my father's death," continued the earl, "this letter was given to me. It was addressed to the Earl of Vauxhall, and I opened it. It seemed to me that it was my plain duty to bring it back to you at once. I alone have read it, and it is as though it had never been written."

He handed her the note and stepped back. She opened it, glanced at its contents, and dropped it on the table by which she stood.

"Yes," she said, "that is the note I sent

him yesterday, and he never got it after all. Poor Lord Vauxhall—he seemed so anxious about it."

"I do not blame him," said the earl. "He had everything staked upon your answer."

"Was it as bad as that," she exclaimed.

"Can you doubt it?" answered the earl.

The girl said nothing, but stood with downcast eyes, nervously pulling the petals from a rose upon the table. The earl, watching her, saw her lips move as if she were trying over words that did not suit her, and he also saw a blush mount slowly from her throat to her temples.

"Lord Vauxhall," she said finally, her words halting, her voice trembling, "We Americans do not know much about these things—we are brought up so differently. We come over here and make dreadful mistakes. I am very much afraid that I am making one now, but if I am, you must forgive me and forget it. If, as you say, my answer was of such importance to your father, perhaps, as you have succeeded him, you might like me to repeat it to *you*. If you wish, you may consider that note to have been written to yourself."

The earl dropped his hat upon the floor and ran toward her, his arms extended. The girl looked up, saw him coming, and with a cry, sprang behind the table. The earl, brought up standing, saw something in the girl's eyes that made him think he had been precipitate. He dropped his arms and began to look foolish.

"Come, now," he said, "is that the way they do things in the States? If you are willing to marry me—"

"Marry you?" gasped the girl.

The earl gazed at her silently, then he took the note from the table and read it aloud:

"*Dear Lord Vauxhall: I have thought it all* "*over by myself, and I have talked it all over* "*with my aunt, and my answer is—yes !*"

He looked up. The girl had her handkerchief to her face.

"Don't cry," he said; "I'm sorry I frightened you. I won't do it again if you're not used to it—I mean—if it is not customary in the States."

The girl took the handkerchief from her face. Her cheeks were scarlet, but there were no tears upon them.

"There," she said, "I haven't laughed out loud yet, but if you don't go pretty soon, I shall break down."

The earl shifted his feet uneasily.

"But how about the letter?" he asked, somewhat sullenly.

"Oh, yes," said the girl, "the letter; I suppose I must explain that Lord Vauxhall was very anxious that I should buy some of the family diamonds. He said his son had ruined him. I promised to give an answer yesterday, and so I wrote that note."

The earl looked about for his hat. It was not to be seen.

"I think," said the girl, "that when you dropped it, it rolled under the sofa. I will ring for a servant to get it for you."

The earl said nothing, but getting on all fours, fished out the hat with the deep mourning band. While he was in this posture the handkerchief went up to the girl's face again, but she made no sound.

When the earl reached the door he turned and bowed again, as though to royalty. The girl still stood behind the table. As he looked at her his eyes began to twinkle and his lips to twitch.

"You may come out of the corner now, little girl, if you will be good," he said, and went out laughing.

When the girl heard the street door close, she came quickly from behind the table and ran to the window. She separated the curtains by an inch and looked out. She saw the Earl of Vauxhall go down the steps and cross the sidewalk to the hansom. As he reached the curb, he turned and looked up. He was still laughing. The girl watched him until he disappeared down the street, then she left the window and walked slowly toward the door.

" I wonder," she said to herself, " what would have happened if that table had not been there."

She stood a moment, wondering; then, blushing and laughing, she grasped her skirts and ran from the room.

The footmen in the hall below heard the flying footsteps and the laughter.

" 'Icks," said the elder, "she lacks repose."

" She do, Mr. Wilson," assented Hicks, "she do."

THE PEACH

THE PEACH

I

BEFORE my uncle turned serious and began to put on flesh, he spent some years in the critical study of mankind, his researches compelling him to divide his time between Paris and Monte Carlo. For purposes of taking deep soundings in the sea of humanity he kept his steam-yacht in the Mediterranean, and it used to be said that the holding-ground on the north shore of that pleasant lake was spoiled by the empty champagne bottles dropped overboard from the *Merry Wives*.

It was during this period of research and experiment that my uncle, very early one morning, kicked open the green baize doors of the Municipal Casino, in Nice, and emerged upon the Place Massena. Had it not been carnival time his

[113]

appearance might have caused remark, since he wore a Pierrot costume of white satin, his face was floured, and his hair was covered by a smoothly fitting skull-cap. At my uncle's heels there followed a troop of male and female maskers who, with shrill cries, besought him not to leave them. Various propositions were advanced,—"one more dance," "a little supper at the London House," "a drive to Cimella to ring up the monks,"—but against all these my uncle, who by this time had entered a cab, turned a smiling but resolute face.

"Ladies and gentlemen," he said in excellent French, waving his hand over the back of the voiture, "and thou especially, Hortense," and he threw a kiss to a tall girl in pink, "it lacerates my heart to leave you. But what would you; we are still young and the world is very small. Count Lenormand, I kiss your hands. Hortense, thy lips. To the harbor, coachman."

The cab started when a young man in

ordinary dress sprang forward and cried, "And me, monsieur?"

"Ah," said my uncle, "I had forgotten,—jump in;" and the two drove off together, followed by cheers, laughing adieus, and perhaps a tear or two, for my uncle had great possessions.

At the harbor the *Merry Wives* lay so close to the quay that one had only to cross the gang-plank to reach her deck.

"Captain Sparrow," said my uncle to the officer who saluted him at the gangway, "this gentleman is so good as to give me a half-hour of his company; after that you may get under way."

If the captain observed anything unusual in his owner's costume he gave no sign, but saluting again he turned on his heel and walked toward the engine-room hatch. The after-deck was covered with rugs and skins. On a large table were two softly shaded lamps, books, and a collection of pipes. Scattered about were several lounging-chairs. My uncle touched a bell and directed the steward who answered it to bring brandy and soda.

"Monsieur," said the young man, "before I partake of your hospitality I should tell you my name;" and he handed my uncle a visiting-card, upon which the latter read by the lamplight the words "Sebastian Grantaire."

"Your name, monsieur," said my uncle, "is a new one to me, and I do not recall your face, but I have an idea that I can guess the affair that gives me the pleasure of your acquaintance. When you spoke to me at the ball I said to myself, 'It has arrived.' It is in behalf of a certain lady that you are here, is it not?"

The stranger shook his head with a smile.

"No, monsieur," he replied, "I bear no challenge."

"I am delighted to see you, monsieur," said my uncle.

"Perhaps," he resumed after a moment's pause, "it is that a cathedral is to be restored, and that an opportunity is afforded?"

"No, monsieur, I have no subscription paper."

"One more guess," said my uncle, "and I am done. It is that a noble family, having met with reverses, is obliged to part with a Rembrandt or a Correggio. Ah, I have it at last."

"You are wrong again, monsieur. I have not come to sell you pictures, but to lay the world at your feet."

"Have you it with you?" asked my uncle.

"Yes," said Grantaire, and putting his hand in his breast he drew forth a small green morocco portfolio, which he placed upon the table.

My uncle eyed it curiously for a moment. "I see that the world is flat," he remarked.

"Monsieur," asked Grantaire, "what is it that all mankind dreads but cannot escape?"

"The police," replied my uncle, promptly.   [117]

"No," said Grantaire, "it is death, and with this," and he placed his hand on the portfolio, "I shall abolish death. Do you desire greater wealth than you already possess? Do you long for power? You shall have such riches as the world never saw heaped up, and such power as never yet man wielded. I have spent fifteen years and a fortune seeking it. Listen a moment. When Miserob the Armenian, early in the fifth century, wished to translate the Bible, he sent his students to Alexandria to learn the Greek tongue. One of them brought this back with him. Miserob gave it to Moses of Khorene, who placed it in the Vatican library in the year 437. When the Popes went to Avignon in 1309 it went with them, and when they returned to Rome, Gregory XI. carried it back. When the Duke of Bourbon sacked the Vatican in 1527, and was shot by Benvenuto Cellini, one of his soldiers stole it, sold it to the royal library at Fontainebleau in 1534, and stole it back again the next day. This soldier caused

[118]

me much trouble, monsieur. He pawned it once in Paris, and twice in Marseilles, under an assumed name, and chancing to die at Corbie in Picardy, the monk who shrived him took it from his bosom. This monk placed it in the library of the monastery, and it appears in the catalogue of 1638. In 1794, it was removed to the town library of Amiens, where it was unnoticed. Four years ago I was made care-taker at Amiens, and day before yesterday I found it. It had been stolen for fourteen hundred years, and I had no scruples. Why should I? It had cost me the best years of my life, and five hundred thousand francs to find it. Who is the rightful owner? The library at Alexandria. Where is that library? Cæsar burned it."

"That was a long time ago, monsieur," remarked my uncle.

"So long," said Grantaire, "that the statute has run. It is mine by right of discovery, and history begins from this day."

My uncle struck a match and lit a pipe.

"Monsieur Grantaire," he asked, "what is *it*?"

The Frenchman sprang from his chair. "Haven't I told you?" he exclaimed; then, leaning over, he whispered in my uncle's ear, "It is a map showing the exact location of the Garden of Eden, and a manuscript by Miserob, who visited it."

Just then Captain Sparrow came aft and asked if he should get under way.

"Does it matter whether you stay here or go on to Monaco?" asked my uncle of Grantaire.

"No," he replied; "the little bag I brought aboard is my luggage."

My uncle nodded to the captain, who gave an order and went upon the bridge. The boatswain's whistle sounded, the crew cast off the hawsers, a bell jingled in the engine-room, the screw began to slowly beat the water, and the *Merry Wives* glided out of the harbor. Just then the sun peeped over the boot of Italy, and the water and the sky turned from gray to pink and then to blue; a faint breeze

sprang up from the east, bringing with it
the scent of roses and of pines, the bugles
sounded from Villafranca, and my uncle
leaned over and blew out the lamps, for
it was morning.

II

WHEN Grantaire came on deck at
four bells the yacht lay at anchor under
the palace of Monaco. An awning had
been stretched over the after-deck, and
under this breakfast was laid. The steward had just placed the melons on the
table when my uncle came up the hatch.

"Ah, monsieur," he said, "I dreamed
of the Garden of Eden all night, and we
wake to find it on our port bow," and
he waved his hand toward Monte Carlo.
"Yes," he continued, as they took their
seats, "here you have sky, water, trees,
flowers, music, pigeon-shooting, gam-
bling, and every two-footed beast that
walks the earth; besides there are no
taxes. Does not that make a paradise?
Why did you spend so much money for

your map when you could have bought
a Baedeker for four francs?"

"Monsieur," replied Grantaire, "I
fear that you do not take me seriously.
Have you a Bible?"

"Steward," said my uncle, "is there a
Bible on board?"

"Yes, sir," replied the steward; "when
we was fittin' in Southampton the mate
won one at a Salvation Army raffle."

"Ask the mate to loan it to me," said
my uncle, "and meanwhile, monsieur,
try these eggs *à la Bercy*."

The steward came back with the book.
Grantaire took it and crossed himself.
"This," he said solemnly, "is the Word
of God."

Then he read the following from the
Book of Genesis:

"*And the Lord God planted a garden east-*
"*ward in Eden, and there he put the man*
"*whom he had formed.*

"*And out of the ground made the Lord God*
"*to grow every tree that is pleasant to the*
"*sight and good for food; the tree of life also*

" *in the midst of the garden, and the tree of*
" *knowledge of good and evil.*
" *And the Lord God commanded the man,*
" *saying, Of every tree of the garden thou*
" *mayest freely eat* ;
" *But of the tree of the knowledge of good and*
" *evil, thou shalt not eat of it : for in the day*
" *that thou eatest thereof thou shalt surely die.*"

He paused a moment and resumed:

" *And the Lord God said, Behold, the man*
" *is become as one of us, to know good and evil;*
" *and now, lest he put forth his hand and take*
" *also of the tree of life, and eat, and live for-*
" *ever :*
" *Therefore the Lord God sent him forth from*
" *the Garden of Eden, to till the ground from*
" *whence he was taken.*
" *So he drove out the man ; and he placed at*
" *the east of the Garden of Eden the Cheru-*
" *bim and the flame of a sword, which turned*
" *every way to keep the way of the tree of*
" *life.*"

He closed the book and said : " Do you
understand now what I have obtained ?

Do you see that what the world has been seeking for ages I have found in a search of only fifteen years? Don't you understand that the man who finds the Garden of Eden will find there growing the Tree of Life, and that he who finds the tree may eat of the fruit thereof?"

My uncle buttered a muffin with great care. "Monsieur," he said at length, "do you believe what you have just read?"

"Yes," replied Grantaire. "My mother taught me to believe it when I was a child, and I have met no man since who was wise enough to give me a substitute. Besides, Miserob found the garden and the tree."

"It does not seem to have worked in his case," said my uncle. "He is quite dead, is he not?"

"Yes, he died fourteen hundred years ago, but he did not eat of the fruit."

"And you, monsieur, if you were to find the tree, would you disobey the divine injunction and eat thereof; would your mother approve of that?"

[124]

"Ah, monsieur," replied Grantaire, "man was told that he might freely eat of every tree in the garden save only of the tree of the knowledge of good and evil. He was not forbidden to eat of the tree of life."

My uncle smoked silently for some minutes; then he said, somewhat abruptly, "Tell me what you wish and why you have come to me."

"Monsieur," said Grantaire, "I wish money for my journey, and I come to you because you are young and venturesome and the richest man of your years in France to-day."

My uncle rose from the table, and the quartermaster, who had been waiting this signal that breakfast was over, hauled down the meal pennant. Grantaire remained in his seat. My uncle took a turn up and down the deck, returned Captain Sparrow's good morning, and then went on the bridge. He came down again and walked aft to where Grantaire was sitting.

"Monsieur," he said, "how much will it cost?"

"As you would travel," replied Grantaire, "with a caravan, bearers, a chef, a valet, and an ice machine, it would take a million francs. As I shall go, a hundred thousand will suffice."

"Have you any money?" asked my uncle.

"Two louis," replied Grantaire; and he laid them on the table.

"They will buy you an umbrella for your journey," said my uncle. "You were wise to come to me, for as you say, I am very, very young. I have also more money than is good for me. I decline to furnish one hundred thousand francs, but I will make you a sporting proposition. I came here this morning to gamble. I have fifty thousand francs in my cabin. I never lose more. I will divide with you, and we will go to Monte Carlo after lunch; if you win seventy-five thousand francs, there you are."

"And if I lose?" asked Grantaire.

"Why, in that event," said my uncle, "there you are also."

At luncheon there were some hot-house peaches on the table. Grantaire took one up and said, "By the way, monsieur, I am convinced that I shall find the fruit to be more like a peach than an apple, which in its palatable form is artificial."

"Excuse me," said my uncle, somewhat impatiently, "but the launch is at the gangway, and if you are ready, I am. Here are the twenty-five thousand francs."

While in the launch, Grantaire said, "This is the nineteenth of the month and my birthday."

They landed just east of the station, and crossing the tracks, mounted the long flight of steps to the terrace. When they entered the casino, Grantaire went into the bureau and asked for a card of admission. He called my uncle's attention to the fact that it was numbered 1906. Then they left their hats and Grantaire's bag in the *vestiaire*. Grantaire's hat check

was number 719. They went into the large
room where the four roulette tables are.

"Good luck to you," said my uncle,
and turned to the left. Grantaire went
toward the table on the right.

"Now," said my uncle to himself, "I'll
give him a chance to bolt and close the
incident."

But Grantaire did not bolt. He took
his stand behind the players until some
one rose to leave, then he threw a louis
on the table and claimed the vacant seat.
My uncle went over and stood where he
could watch him. Grantaire handed the
croupier two notes for 1,000 francs each
and received the gold for them. Then he
placed eight louis on the number nineteen, and 1,200 francs on the line between
nineteen and twenty-two, thus playing the
"transverse." He next laid 3,000 francs
on the middle dozen. The croupiers and
the players began to watch him. Next he
placed 6,000 francs on "red," the same
on "passe," and the same on "impaire";
the remainder, 2,620 francs, he laid in

the square at the bottom of the first column of figures. The croupiers unfolded
the notes and called their amounts. The
players from the other tables crowded
about, and my uncle had hard work to
keep his place.

"Make your play, ladies and gentlemen," called the croupier, then, after a
moment's pause, he spun the wheel and
threw the ball. There was silence until
the ball began to hit against the partitions
of the slowing wheel. "Nothing more
goes," called the croupier, and then the
seconds became hours. Suddenly the click
of the ball ceased—it had settled into one
of the partitions. "Dix-neuf, passe, impaire et rouge," called the croupier. Grantaire sat unmoved while the croupiers
counted out his several bets; and when
they finally pushed over to him 41,890
francs, he gathered them up, but left his
stakes upon the table and added to them
from his winnings sufficient to cover the
other "transverse," the "corners," the
"couples," and the "cross," and he also

completed his stake upon the first column.

No one else made a bet. The croupier bowed to Grantaire and asked, "Is monsieur quite ready?"

"Quite," replied Grantaire, and the wheel started. There was the same strained silence, broken only by the clicking of the ball; and when that ceased, before the croupier could announce the result the crowd shouted. The ball had stopped in number nineteen. The croupier counted out to Grantaire 78,650 francs. He gathered up all the money on the table and left his seat. He walked into the entrance-hall and consulted a railway time-table which hung on one of the pillars. My uncle joined him there.

"Ah, monsieur," said Grantaire, "a train leaves for the East in six minutes. I have won 120,540 francs. I return you the 25,000 which you so kindly loaned me, and the 20,540 as interest," and he thrust a roll of notes into my uncle's hand. They walked toward the station.

"Monsieur," said my uncle, "I ad-

mired your courage when you left your
stake upon the table."

Grantaire took off his hat. "It was
nothing," he said, "compared with yours
when you loaned me the 25,000 francs.
May I ask why you have never asked to
see the map?"

My uncle laughed. "I was afraid," he
answered, "that if I saw it I should go
with you."

Just then the engine whistled, and the
two men shook hands.

"I shall report to you in New York,"
said Grantaire, and ran down the steps.

III

EIGHT years afterward, on an afternoon in early June, the *Merry Wives*
passed Whitestone bound west. The yacht,
being feminine, had changed her name,
and was now the *Beatrix*. Captain Sparrow was on the bridge, and my uncle was
dozing in a steamer chair under the after
awning. On the table, among the books
and flowers, lay a pair of small gloves and

a fan. A green parrot hung in a gilded cage.

"Jack," came a voice from the after hatch. My uncle smiled and half opened his eyes.

"Here," he replied.

"Jack," the voice continued, "throw me down your keys."

My uncle fished his key-ring out of his trousers pocket and tossed it down the hatch ; then he resumed his slumbers, but not for long, for soon there emerged from the companionway a white sailor hat, then a comely, smiling face, then a blue serge gown, and finally, as my aunt stepped onto the deck, a white shoe and a few inches of black silk stocking.

"Jack," she said, "see what I found in the little drawer in your dressing-table," and she held out a visiting-card to which were pinned a number of French bank-notes. "Who is Sebastian Grantaire?"

"I declare," said my uncle, "I had forgotten all about it," and he took the notes from my aunt and counted them. "Twen-

ty thousand five hundred," he said. Then
he took a small purse from his pocket,
from which he abstracted two louis.
"These," he said, "go with them and
make up the 20,540 francs." And then
he told my aunt the story.

"Jack," said she, "it seems to me that
you did very strange things when you
were studying in Europe."

"Nothing," replied he, "to what I
have done since."

"What?" asked my aunt.

"There's my total reformation, for one
thing," said my uncle, who grew demon-
strative.

"Don't," said my aunt, straightening
her hat, "some of the men will see
you."

"They don't mind," said my uncle, and
he did it again.

When the *Beatrix* dropped her anchor
off the yacht-station at Twenty-sixth
Street, my uncle and my aunt went ashore
in the gig, and were met at the float by
a servant who, as he shut the door of the

[133]

brougham, handed in a bundle of letters.
My uncle opened the first one, read it,
settled back into the corner, and dropped
the hand which held the paper onto his
knee. My aunt, who had been looking
out of her window, surprised him in this
attitude.

"What is it, Jack?" she asked.

My uncle handed her the letter. It was
in French, and she read it aloud:

" *If Monsieur will take the Elevated Railway*
" *this evening and will descend at* 155*th Street*
" *as if to proceed to the Polo Grounds, he will*
" *learn the gratitude of*

"SEBASTIAN GRANTAIRE.

" *Friday, June fourth.*"

They sat silent for some moments, then
my aunt drew close to my uncle and said,
"Jack, I'm afraid; just think, we were
talking of him only an hour ago, and you
had not thought of him before in eight
years; and now the first thing you get
when you reach home is his letter, and
he wants you to go way up to the Polo

Grounds to-night. Shall you go, Jack?"

"Of course I shall," he replied, "and I'll have Grantaire in to lunch to-morrow. Perhaps you can get on to his game—he's too deep for me."

This tribute to my aunt's superior astuteness silenced her objections, and my uncle went down the steps of the Elevated at 155th Street that evening at just six minutes past nine and started to walk toward Eighth Avenue. He had not gone far when a shadow clambered down from the rocks and stood in the road until my uncle came up; then the shadow raised its hat and said, "Monsieur, I felt sure that you would come."

"Grantaire," asked my uncle, somewhat nervously, "is that you?"

"Ah, monsieur," replied the shadow, "that opens a philosophical question which has baffled the ages. There are good things to be said on both sides of it; and to be frank with you, I don't know. I only know that eight years ago you loaned me 25,000 francs, and if I

were Grantaire then I am Grantaire now,
but who knows? Come."

They turned off from the road across
the rocks.

"Where are you going?" asked my
uncle.

"But a step," replied Grantaire; "my
house is yonder."

In a few moments they stopped at one
of those composite huts found only in the
upper part of Manhattan Island. While
Grantaire was working at the lock my
uncle looked about him and saw over at
the south the illuminated tents of "The
Greatest Show on Earth" pitched on the
Polo Grounds, and the faint breeze
brought to his ears the music of the
circus. Grantaire entered the hut and
turned up the lamp. My uncle followed
him, and then for the first time saw his
companion's face. Grantaire was an old
man. His hair and beard were white, his
flesh had wasted and turned yellow, and
his eyes were only glittering black beads,
without pupil or iris, that rested on my

uncle for an instant and then turned away.

"Monsieur," said Grantaire, his eyes averted, his fingers ceaselessly playing upon the arms of his chair, "to-night I am in a position to repay the loan you made me."

"You forget," said my uncle, "that you paid it to me the same day at Monte Carlo, and left with me in addition 20,540 francs, which I now return to you." And he placed them on the table.

"As you please," said Grantaire, "they will help to pay postage. To-morrow, when my secret is known, I shall have a correspondence. When I said that I was in a position to repay your loan I did not mean that I actually had the money; I meant that I had the power to command money. I have found the Tree of Life. Shall I tell you where I found it?"

My uncle thought a moment and then said, "No; tell me what you found. Don't tell me your route. If I knew that, I might wake some morning with an irresistible desire to travel."

"I found," said Grantaire, "after a six months' journey over mountain-ranges and across deserts, two small volcanoes that were marked upon my map as the 'Cherubim with the Flaming Sword,' and traversing a short valley which lay between them I entered the Garden of Eden. I spent three years in that sweet spot as the trusted guest of a tribe of grave and gentle men whose whole world is bounded by the hills which circle them. All beyond is, to them, the desert.

"In the midst of the garden is a group of small trees which is guarded night and day. The fruit is never touched, and where it falls it lies. No one ever enters the grove except the chief, or high priest, and his family. I need not tell you that those trees are the descendants of the Tree of Life, but the inhabitants of the garden do not know it. All that they know is that their fathers, from time immemorial, have guarded the grove, and that, for some reason, it is sacred.

"For three years I lived in the shadow

[138]

of the trees, but I never passed the line of guards which encircled them. Then, one night in the autumn of the fourth year, when the ripe fruit had begun to fall, I stole away from the valley, passed the Cherubim and the Flaming Sword, which seemed to menace me, and once more crossed the desert that separates Eden from the world."

"And the Tree of Life," cried my uncle—"you did not eat of it after all?"

"No," answered Grantaire, "I have never tasted of it, but I shall to-night, and so shall you."

He took up the lamp, crossed the room to a door, opened it, and my uncle followed him into a rudely constructed hothouse, framed with scantling, and covered with the glass sash which market gardeners use for their frames.

The glass was thickly whitewashed. There was a stove at one end; and a litter of matting, straw, and broken packing-boxes covered the floor. In the centre stood a large wooden box painted green, and in the box a tree about four feet high was growing.

My uncle had scarcely time to note these things when he heard Grantaire say something in a strange language, and a woman came out of the shadow and stood in the light. She was clothed in some graceful, flowing garment, her hands were crossed upon her breast, and her yellow hair hung about her waist. My uncle had not known that the world possessed anything so beautiful. She stood a moment, knelt at my uncle's feet, and then went back to her seat in the shadow.

"I told her," said Grantaire, "that you and she are the only friends I have in the world. You may speak freely; she knows only her own tongue."

"Who is she?" my uncle whispered.

Grantaire did not reply at once. Finally he said: "She is Lilith, the daughter of the high priest. She took the fruit after I had besought her for two years, and she came across the desert with me. Do you think the good God will ever forgive me?

She brought away two of the fruit, and I planted the pits when we reached Marseilles. I was right, you see; the tree is more like a peach than an apple. Both of the pits sprouted and grew until we were half-way across the Atlantic, then one of them died. Lilith and I have watched the other every moment during the last four years, turn and turn about, and I have asked you to come here to-night, for it has borne fruit and the fruit is ripe. I have beggared myself, spent twenty-three years of my life, and"—glancing toward the form in the shadow—"have been a scoundrel, but I have gained immortality. Why should I bother about my soul if it is never to leave my body, and what can happen to my body when death shall have no more dominion over me?"

"I never exactly understood," said my uncle, "how this fruit is to secure to you what you claim. How will it make you rich? How will it give you power? Of course, you can start a cannery, but—"

Grantaire turned on him. "What would

you give me if the young wife, which the newspapers say you have taken, were dying and I could save her life? Multiply that sum by half the population of the earth, and what do you get? How much would the French Government have paid me in 1870 if I could then have made her soldiers proof against the German bullets? How much would the life insurance companies of the world give me to render all their risks a nullity? And as for power— is there any limit to him who holds life and death in his hand, and who can make the history of the world? Come," he cried, "the harvest is ripe; let us eat."

He walked toward the tree, still carrying the lamp. My uncle followed, and among the shining leaves saw a highly colored fruit, somewhat oblong in shape, and very like a peach. Grantaire stood a moment holding the lamp above his head and peering about the room as though dreading interruption. The lamp shook and flared. Finally he reached his hand toward the fruit, but drew it back again, and taking his handkerchief from his pocket he wiped his forehead. Then he muttered to himself: "And now, lest he put forth his hand and take also of the Tree of Life, and eat and live forever"—and then he thrust out his hand quickly and plucked the fruit.

A low moan came from the woman crouched in the shadow. Grantaire, still carrying the lamp, walked over to her and offered her the fruit. She shuddered, drew back, and hid her face in her hands. With a shrug of his shoulders, Grantaire came back and held out the fruit to my uncle, who put his hands behind him and shook his head.

"Coward!" hissed Grantaire; "most men fear to die—it appears that you are afraid to live;" and he raised the fruit to his lips.

Just then there was a faint rustling in the straw at the foot of the tree. Grantaire heard it and glanced down, and my uncle, who was watching his face, saw it suddenly grow gray.

[143]

Then my uncle looked down also and saw slowly gliding out from the straw a little green and black field snake that twined itself about the stem of the tree.

"Look!" screamed Grantaire. "Satan, who tempted man aforetime to lose his soul, is here to see he does not win it back again!" And he flung the lamp, with all his force, straight at the glistening coil.

There was a crash — silence — and then all was fire. My uncle put his arms across his face and burst through the glass. Burned and cut, he turned and saw for a moment that Grantaire was bending over the tree, evidently trying to shield it with his body, and that the woman was kneeling at his feet, her arms clasped about his knees. Then the roof fell in, the flames shot up, and my uncle saw no more.

Some days after, my uncle, plastered and bandaged, opened his eyes upon the sweet face of my aunt, who was bending over him.

"What is it?" he asked faintly.

"You have been badly hurt," she replied. "You were burned and—"

"Oh, yes," he said, "I remember now."

Then in a moment he whispered, "Poor Grantaire! I found paradise nearer home,"—and he raised my aunt's hand to his lips.

THE SENIOR READER

THE SENIOR READER

I

WHEN in May, 1857, Mr. Anthony Panizzi—he had not then been knighted—opened the great reading-room of the British Museum, he walked down the centre aisle with the Prince Consort and the trustees, and spoke to a man in a shabby coat who stood near the door.

"Mr. Basilwood," said Panizzi, "you are my senior reader, since you have already been twenty years in Burlington House, and you shall have the choice of seats. I hope," he added, "that *this* building will stand until your great work is finished."

"Who is that?" whispered the Prince.

"Sir," answered Panizzi, "that is William Basilwood. Much learning hath made him mad."

"Dear me!" said the Prince.

"Quite so," said Panizzi.

Basilwood smiled at the use of such colloquial English by a German and an Italian, but said nothing, and going up the aisle, took the first desk on the right, the desk which he was to occupy for forty years. He sent in his list of books, and was just getting to work when he heard his name spoken at his shoulder. He turned, annoyed by the interruption, and saw the Prince.

"I beg you not to rise," said the latter. "Let me sit by you a moment. The oldest reader in the Museum will doubtless take pity upon my ignorance, since I have observed that knowledge breeds urbanity. Tell me about your work, and I will try to understand."

"Sir," said Basilwood, gruffly, "I am seeking the basis of human life."

"Ah," said the Prince, "I am German bred and simple, and I have been taught that life is the breath of God."

"Perhaps," replied Basilwood, "but it is not proven."

[150]

The Prince sat silent for a moment, and then he asked, softly, "Must all things be proven? Is there no such thing as faith?"

"Sir," exclaimed Basilwood, "when you speak to a scientific man of 'faith,' you insult his intelligence. While he is striving to present the race with facts, you ask him to compromise on fables. I grant you there are things so trivial that the absolute truth concerning them is not worth the trouble of its establishment. I have faith that you are the husband of our Gracious Queen, although I was not present at the marriage ceremony. But who, except the Queen, cares whether you are or not? If it were proven, would bread be cheaper, would life be easier, would death be sweeter?"

The Prince flushed and half rose; then he caught himself, resumed his seat, and, after a moment, said,—

"Pardon me, Mr. Basilwood. I should not have interrupted your work. I told you I was simply bred. I spoke of faith as simple people do who rely upon others to tell them the great truths which they themselves are incapable of finding out. I come to you, who for twenty years have lived with books, and ask you to give me the drop of attar which you have extracted from their leaves. It is much to ask, but life is much to me. You have already forgotten that I am the Prince Consort; forget that I am anything save one who seeks knowledge. Can you blame a thirsty man because he runs to the fountain, and perhaps stumbles as he runs?"

At this Basilwood bowed, for he had once possessed manners, and said, "Sir, as yet I have but a theory."

"And I have many," said the Prince, laughing. "Tell me yours."

"Have you time?" asked Basilwood.

"I have fifteen minutes," the Prince answered, looking at his watch; "after that I must leave to open a morgue or a flower-show,—I have forgotten which comes first."

"I can tell you all my facts in less time than that," said Basilwood.

[152]

"And you have read for twenty years?" exclaimed the Prince.

"Yes," replied Basilwood, "but much that I have read was written upon 'faith,' and does not count."

The Prince glanced at his companion out of the corner of his eye, but said nothing.

"A child is born into the world," resumed Basilwood, "well-formed, lusty, and crying."

"Yes," exclaimed the Prince, "I can vouch for the crying. Have you children, Mr. Basilwood?"

"I believe so, sir," replied Basilwood, "but I do not charge my mind with such matters, and I must look to make sure."

He took a worn memorandum-book from his pocket, turned some of its leaves, and then exclaimed:

"Of course I have a child, Margaret. Here is the entry." And he read from the book:

"*January* 3, 1857. *Museum bought copy*

[153]

"*of Wicked Bible from Stevens for eighteen*
"*guineas. In case 24a, 41. Daughter born.*"

"That proves it," he said, closing the book. "Margaret is my daughter, and she was born January 3, 1857."

"Dear me!" exclaimed the Prince.

"That is what you remarked when Panizzi told you I was mad," said Basilwood.

"But we left that new-born child crying," said the Prince, quickly. "Should we not return to it?"

"That child has life in him," resumed Basilwood. "He is 'quick,' as they used to say, and as the law-writers say now. The question is, Where is the seat of life? In a week his nurse bites off his finger-nails so that they may grow thin. He still lives. Soon they cut his hair. He does not miss it. As he grows older he loses a foot, a leg, an arm, and still he lives. The seat of life has not been overturned. Then we come to what are vulgarly called 'the vital organs,' and we find that a man has lived with a crowbar driven through his

[154]

brain, with a bullet through the heart, with the lungs eaten up, with the bowels perforated, with the stomach removed. Where is the centre of vitality? Where is the pin-point in the human frame that death touches to stop the working mechanism which we call life? If we can find it, perhaps we can guard it."

"Mr. Basilwood," said the Prince, rising, "I fear that my time is up, but there is one fact that I can give you, and that is, that the heart is not the seat of life. I know a man, a strong man, one who helps to make the laws of this realm, who eats and sleeps and walks and talks—yes, he talks a great deal, and yet he has no heart at all."

"That must be Colonel Sibthorp," said Basilwood, with a chuckle. "The papers say that he cut your allowance in the Commons from fifty to thirty thousand pounds."

The Prince smiled and held out his hand. "Good-by," he said, "and be sure to send me the first eleven copies of your

[155]

work. That will be one each for the Queen, myself, and the children."

"The breath of God, indeed," said Basilwood to himself as the Prince walked away. "I have lost half an hour." And he fell to his work.

II

FOR some years Basilwood was known at the Museum as "the man that the Prince spoke with;" then one morning a charming girl of eighteen led him slowly up the aisle, took off his wraps, found his spectacles, put a shilling in his pocket, kissed him, and, smiling, went away. In the evening she came to fetch him, and from that day he was spoken of by the doorkeepers, the messengers, the confirmed readers, and even by Sir Anthony himself, as "Margaret's father."

One evening she was a little late, and came into the Museum with cheeks aglow and eyes sparkling.

"Daddy," she whispered, as with eager fingers she helped him gather up his notes, "this has been the most beautiful day of my life. You love me, don't you, dear?" and she pushed the white hair back from his forehead and kissed him. They took an omnibus and crossed to the Surrey side. She held his hand the whole way and did not speak, but her face was as that of an angel.

At dinner she was very talkative. "Daddy," she said, after a short pause, "how old was my mother when you and she were married?"

Basilwood did not answer.

"Was she very beautiful?" she asked.

"Yes," he replied, "and you are very like her."

Her cheeks flamed, and springing up she ran over to him and put her arms about his neck.

"Oh, I am so glad," she cried. "I wish to be very beautiful indeed."

"Your mother," said Basilwood, "was a good woman, but she died during the week that the Offer library was sold at Southby's. I missed two days of the sale."

There was a knock at the door, and Margaret ran to it, opened it, and went out. There was whispering in the hall, and then in walked a strapping young fellow with a flower in his button-hole and the light of love in his eyes.

"Ah, Mr. Basilwood," he said, holding out his hand; "how goes the Great Work?"

"Sir," said Basilwood, "who the devil are you?"

The question seemed to faze the young man, but only for a moment.

"Don't you know me?" he said. "I am Philip Kennet, for whom you stood godfather down in Berkshire, twenty odd years ago; and I have been to see your daughter and you ever so many times, and have read no end of copy for you, and I love Margaret and she loves me. Will you give her to me, Mr. Basilwood?"

Then Margaret came in and found the men confronting each other.

"Who is this man?" asked Basilwood.

"Oh, father," said Margaret, "is it as

[158]

bad as that?" And she went to him and took his hand.

"Philip, dear," she said to the young man, who was no longer smiling, "he does n't remember even you. You see how impossible it is that I should leave him."

"Leave him!" he cried; "I don't ask you to leave him. There will be always a place for him. Only give me the right to take care of you both. He shall have all the books he wants. Why should you be slaving in that shop when I—"

She put her hand over his mouth.

"Margaret," asked Basilwood, "is this true?"

"Is what true, father?"

"That this is Sir George Kennet's son?"

"Yes, father."

"And has he been here often, as he says?"

She smiled sadly and replied, "Yes, very often."

"And do you love him?"

She blushed, but answered bravely, "I love him next to you."

[159]

"Then, sir," said Basilwood, "I hope I know how to be unselfish, and if all goes well, you may have her on the day my book is finished."

III

IT was Jubilee year and a dreary day in December. Basilwood left his desk at one o'clock and went to the Museum restaurant. He walked very slowly and leaned heavily upon his stick. When he had taken the chair which a waiter placed for him, he drew a parcel from his pocket, opened it, and began to eat his bread and cheese.

A little man, made noticeable by a large watch-chain and a brown wig, came in, looked nervously about the room, and then came over to the senior reader.

"Mr. Basilwood," he asked, "do you happen to know much about twins?"

Basilwood shook his head.

"Well," continued the stranger, "I can tell you this much. The life of a twin is hell upon earth. What's that you are eating,—bread and cheese? Join me in a pork pie. They are very good here. Waiter, a pork pie and two mugs of bitter."

They took their seats at a table behind the door.

"Mr. Basilwood," resumed the stranger, "I am told that you are the senior reader in the Museum, and that you have given more than sixty years to the preparation of a work upon the physical basis of life. My name is Gilbert, Theodore Gilbert, and if ever a man needed counsel, I'm the man."

"What can I do for you?" asked Basilwood.

"You can have another pint of bitter," replied Gilbert.

"Granted," said Basilwood.

"My father," continued Gilbert, "when he died, left three things behind that raised the devil. He left twins and a home-made will. The will said that David—that's my brother—and I were to have three thousand a year each until one of us died, and then the survivor was to have the pot, a million or more. That made quite a race, and, being twins, we started even. We lived together for a time in the old house, but it finally got onto our nerves. It is no sport to dine with a man when you stand between him and a million. We used to carve by turns, and sometimes we would exchange plates and then match a coin to determine which should take the first mouthful. I used to have my tooth-powder analyzed every Monday. After a year or two, this got to be a bit dreary. One night I went into the dining-room early, and there was David with the salt-cellar in one hand and a little blue-paper parcel in the other. When he saw me he turned as white as his shirt and threw the blue paper into the grate. Then he stood and grinned. He did n't speak. He simply grinned. I was at him in a moment with the carving-knife, and I slashed him across the face. He went down, and his head hit the

[162]

base-board. He bled beautifully. In a week he came down-stairs with a black plaster from the corner of his nose to his chin.

"'There, damn you,' I cried, 'they can tell us apart now.'

"'I 've had enough of this,' he said, and we parted. He went to San Francisco, in America, and I stayed here. When he went out of the house he turned and shook his fist at me.

"'Curse you,' he said, 'I 'll outlive you.'

"'Not if there is anything in early hours and dry feet,' I replied, and I took a cab for Sir Andrew Ashley's. He's the chap that used to tend the Queen when she was strengthening the succession. I told him about the will and about my twin brother, and then I asked him plump, 'What are my chances?'

"He played with his glasses a moment and then went to the door.

"'William,' he said to the footman, 'if the Chief Justice calls, beg him to wait. I cannot be disturbed.'

"When I heard this, I fished about in my pocket for three more sovereigns.

"'Mr. Gilbert,' he said, when he had resumed his seat, 'a curious law governs double births. Twins are apt to resemble each other not only in features and disposition, but also in constitution. They are like two watches of the same make, which, if wound up together, will run down together. So I say to you, putting aside accidents and acute diseases, the chances are that you and your brother will die about the same time. I trust this is satisfactory. Good morning, Mr. Gilbert. It looks like rain.'

"I went the rounds of the doctors, and they all told me the same thing. 'You and your brother will die at the same time.' About ten years ago I came here in the hope that I could learn something from the books. I have read more than a thousand, but have found nothing that tells me how to live. Oh, sir, in all your sixty years of research, have you hit upon the secret of life?"

[164]

Basilwood rose slowly and leaned upon the back of his chair.

"Mr. Gilbert," he said, with great deliberation, "it is written that reading makes a full man. I have read sixty years, and on top of that I have now two pints of bitter. I am very full. I will see you to-morrow."

"One moment," said Gilbert. "Having exhausted the doctors and literature, last night I tried the fakirs. I went to the Hindoo in Gower Street. He came over for the Jubilee. He told me I might ask him one question, and I said, 'Tell me the date of my death.'

"He laughed and said, 'I feared you would ask me some hard question, something about a woman. You have a twin brother. You will both die at the same instant. If you look at your left forearm you will see the date of your death.'"

"Well," said Basilwood, "what did you find?"

Gilbert stripped up his sleeve, and on the white flesh of his arm, in scarlet letters, were the words, "January first, 1897."

Basilwood dipped the corner of his napkin in his water-glass and scrubbed the letters. They only became brighter.

"No go," said Gilbert. "I've tried everything, from Pear's soap to sapolio."

Then his whole manner changed suddenly.

"Oh, Mr. Basilwood," he cried, "I am going to die in ten days. I came to you as a last resort. You can't help me to live, it seems. You can help me to die. I have sat near you for ten years. Sit by me the last night of my life. It is awful to drift out beyond the horizon all alone. You have your daughter. I have watched her for years. I have seen her change from a laughing girl to a woman with white hairs above her temples. I have seen her give her life, her hope, her love to you, and some day she will close your eyes. But I must die alone, unless you come and sit by me. I will promise to die like a gentleman. I'll make no fuss, but it will help me when I pass the line

[166]

and sink, sink to God knows where, if I see a hand of some one of my race waving me a farewell."

Basilwood cleared his throat.

" Mr. ——, excuse me, but your name has escaped me,"—and then he lurched a bit and caught his chair,—" I am the senior reader here—I have read for sixty years—the Prince Consort spoke to me in fifty-seven. He spoke nonsense, but I felt his royal breath on my ear—the divine afflatus—I have written eighteen parts of my work, and I have a notion that the nineteenth part would fit your case. Can't you postpone your death about a year?" And he leaned over his chair and moistened his lips with his tongue.

Then Margaret came into the restaurant.

"Oh, daddy," she cried. "How you frightened me. I feared you had gone home alone."

Basilwood braced himself between his stick and the chair and smiled vacantly. Gilbert came up to Margaret and took off his hat. [167]

"My dear young lady," he said, "your father has promised to spend the last night of the year with me. Here is my address." And he gave her an envelope.

IV

On the afternoon of December 31 Margaret came to the Museum rather earlier than usual. She brought a hand-bag with her, and she reminded her father that they were to pass the night with Mr. Gilbert. "He says in his letter," she explained, "that we are to go to Green-wich and dine at the 'Ship.' We are to have the very best dinner we can order, and we are to drink his health in a bottle of champagne. There was a five-pound note in the letter 'for his treat,' he says. After dinner we are to take a cab and drive to his house, which is in Black-heath, just beyond the Observatory."

They went by boat to Greenwich, and they had their dinner at the "Ship." The fire in the grate, the lights, the clear tur-tle, the turbot, the pheasant in a casserole, the forced asparagus, the vintage wine, the toasted cracker, and the gorgonzola, the demi-tasse, the petit-verre, the long, dark perfecto, and the waiter made havoc with the five-pound note.

"Margaret," said Basilwood, "when 'The Work' is finished, we shall dine like this every night, and if there is anything you wish you shall have it. You know me. I've never denied you anything yet, have I?"

She looked away, and then she said, "No, daddy, you have been very sweet to me." But as she spoke, her hands went up to her face, and she rose quickly and crossed over to the window.

The waiter went out and closed the door softly.

"What's the matter?" asked Basilwood; "does the smoke bother you?"

"No," she said presently, but without turning. "Here is the cab. We must be going."

After a drive of ten minutes they stopped while a gate was opened; then

[169]

they went on, up a driveway bordered by pines, and stopped before the house. The front door opened, and an elderly woman came quickly down the steps.

"Is this Mr. Basilwood and his daughter?" she asked.

"Yes," replied Margaret.

"Thank God," exclaimed the woman, and she led them into the house.

"You are to go up at once," she said to Basilwood, "and the young lady is to stay here with me. He is in the room at the top of the stairs. The first door. You can't miss it. I am the housekeeper."

Basilwood went slowly up the stairs and knocked with his stick on the first door.

"Come in," cried a shrill voice, and Basilwood turned the knob.

Gilbert was in bed, propped up by the pillows. His wig was off and his bald head resembled a huge egg. His cheeks and temples were sunken, but his eyes were unpleasantly bright. His baldness rendered his ears unduely prominent. A black plaster made a line from the corner of his nose down under his chin. His hands lay outside the bedclothes, and the sleeve of his left arm being rolled up, Basilwood could see the scarlet letters which formed the words "January first, 1897," and instinctively he glanced at the clock on the mantel.

"Plenty of time," cried Gilbert; "the clock is right; I set it this noon by the Observatory time-ball. I've got two hours and a half yet before I let go and float off to meet brother David somewhere in the blue. The evening papers are on the table, with the whiskey and the cigars. Did you bring your slippers? Never mind —mine are by the bed. Put them on and make yourself comfortable."

Basilwood mixed himself a glass of grog, and while he was busied with it he heard a chuckle from the bed.

He turned quickly. "What is there to laugh at?" he demanded.

Gilbert's chuckle grew to a laugh, and then to a shout. His face turned purple, and the tears rolled down his cheeks.

"Stop it," cried Basilwood. "It is n't decent for a man in your situation to carry on like that. Stop it, I say, or I will leave you."

"Oh," gasped Gilbert, "it's great. To think of the time and money I have wasted on the doctors, the library, diet, and a quiet life, and then to have the solution of the whole matter pop into my mind this morning while I was shaving! When a thing comes to you like that, it makes you jump. I slashed myself with the razor just as I cut David with the carving-knife. They won't be able, after all, to tell us apart in the hereafter."

Basilwood shortened his stick in his hand and came up to the bed.

"If you have the secret," he hissed, "you had better tell it to me, or you will never see midnight."

Gilbert began to laugh again. "Put up your stick," he said presently. "My truth is like all truths, very simple. I am to die on January 1, 1897, just as the day begins; and David is to die at the same instant; but when will that be for him in San Francisco? It will be four o'clock yesterday afternoon. He will die in 1896 and I in 1897. Which of us will be the survivor? Which of us will get the pot? Damn him, I'll beat him by a year."

"It's a queer thing," he continued, "that the meridian of Greenwich passes through the hall of this house, and this room is the birthplace of the days."

Basilwood went back to his seat and took up his glass.

"If I understand you, Mr. Gilbert," he said, "life is simply a question of longitude?"

"No," replied Gilbert. "The date of your death is a question of longitude. Life itself is the breath of God."

"Where have I heard that before?" said Basilwood, musingly. There was silence in the chamber for some time, and then Gilbert spoke.

"Will you let your daughter come up here for a few moments, and will you step

into the hall when she comes? I have
something to say to her."

Basilwood went to the door and called
Margaret. She came running up the
stairs. As she entered the room, her father left it.

She stood staring at the apparition in
the bed.

"Miss Basilwood," said Gilbert, "I
am sorry to put you to all this bother,
but I have very little time and I wish
to tell you something. Please be seated."

She shook her head and took a step
toward the door.

"For ten years I have seen you, on each
open day, bring your father to the Museum. I have followed you to your home
across the river, and, forgive me, I have
followed you to the shop."

Margaret came forward swiftly. "You
won't tell him how hard I work?" she
whispered, pointing toward the door.

"No, my dear," said Gilbert, "but I
wish that I had my hat on so that I
might take it off to you."

[174]

Margaret smiled.

"That's right," said Gilbert. "I never saw you smile before. It becomes you. I hope that from this on you will smile very often. I shall die to-night, and I have made my will. I have left to you a fortune which I never had. I hope that it will bring happiness to you. I wish that I had known you when I was a young man. If I had, I should not be so uncertain where I am to go at midnight. I should like it if you would say 'good-by' to me; just those words would help me very much when I cross the border."

Margaret came to the bedside and put out her hand.

"Good-by," she said.

"There, there," said Gilbert, "I've made you cry when I wished to make you happy. Go, now, and ask your father to come."

Margaret left the room and Basilwood came in.

"I have almost two hours yet," said Gilbert, "and I think that I will take a nap, but you must certainly wake me just before twelve. I want to see the end of this thing."

He lay back on the pillows and fell asleep instantly.

Basilwood took his seat by the fire and mixed another glass of grog. He sipped it slowly, and when it was finished, his head fell forward and he, too, slept. He was awakened by the striking of the clock. Gilbert was sitting up in bed counting the strokes. When he reached twelve he paused a moment, then he cried, "Ah, David, my lad, is that you? Have you been waiting long? What did you have in that blue paper?"

Then his hands flew up, and he fell back on the pillows.

Basilwood stood at the foot of the bed. Gilbert's left arm lay across his breast. The scarlet letters began to fade away to pink, to lavender, to nothing. When they had entirely disappeared, Basilwood glanced at the clock. It was five minutes past twelve. He opened the window, blew out the candle, drained his glass, and then went slowly down the stairs.

V

FOR a fortnight Basilwood kept away from the Museum; then he returned to his desk and his occupation. At the luncheon hour he walked slowly and with difficulty to the newspaper room in the wing. He consulted a file of the San Francisco *Chronicle* and carried the issue of January 1 back to his desk, as his privilege permitted.

When he had taken his seat, he looked at the index on the first page of the pader, and then turned to the "Death Notices." The first was this:

"*Gilbert. Suddenly, on the afternoon of De-*
"*cember* 31, *David Gilbert, aged sixty-four*
"*years. New York papers please copy.*"

"My God," he exclaimed, "the man was right!"

He sat for a long time motionless and with closed eyes. Then he opened his

[177]

desk and took out the notes for his book which had accumulated during the last few months. He ran them slowly over.

"Sixty years of work," he muttered, "and all wrong."

He began tearing the slips into small pieces. It took some time to tear them all, and the litter nearly filled the desk. He closed the lid and then, taking a large sheet of the Museum paper, he wrote:

"To

HER MAJESTY THE QUEEN:

"*The Prince Consort was right. Life is the* "*Breath of God.*

WILLIAM BASILWOOD,
Senior Reader."

At five o'clock a hansom stopped before the Museum gate and a woman and a man got out. She was dressed in black, with white collar and wrist-bands, the livery of the shop. Her hair was tinged with gray, but there was a charming color in her cheeks, and her eyes were sparkling. The man was bearded and deeply

[178]

tanned, and so tall that he leaned a trifle that his companion might take his arm.

"Philip," she said, as they passed the gate, "I have prayed for this without ceasing, but the book is not yet finished."

"Book or no book, I shall not go away again," he replied.

They went up the steps and through the hall. At the entrance to the reading-room she left him.

"Don't speak to father when he comes out, dear," she said. "He won't know you, and perhaps won't even notice you," and then she went in.

"Good evening, miss," said the door-keeper. "You are a bit late. There he is, sound asleep at his desk, waiting for you."

She went quickly up the aisle, smiling and nodding to one or two that she knew, and put her hand on her father's shoulder.

"Come, daddy," she said ; but he did not move, and so she shook his arm gently. "It is time to go home, daddy," she said, and she leaned over and looked into his face.

A woman's cry rang through the vast room which is sacred to silence.

The senior reader had already gone home.

The Great Work was finished.

SOME OLD FAMILIES

SOME OLD FAMILIES

I

HIGH up in the West Virginia mountains, close to the Kentucky line, is the flag-station Catamount. Here a lumber company has built a great saw-mill, a planing-mill, dry-kilns, and twenty white cottages for the superintendent, the land-looker, the sawyer, the storekeeper, and the other head men. Across the bridge, which spans the Tug River, are the boarding-houses and the dwellings of the four hundred hands, all of whom are more or less white. No black labor is employed. One man performs the duties of telegraph operator and station agent. His name is Bill. He was born in war times, when there was much confusion, and he never had a surname. His account at the store reads, "Bill, Dr."

One night, early in November, Bill

came out of his cabin by the track. As he stood on the platform he faced the river, the mountains, covered with timber to their summits, and the full, round moon which topped them and sent a shiver of silver across the sluggish stream.

"God," said Bill, as he stretched his arms and yawned, "I wisht I was rich."

As there was no response from the bridge, the white cottages, the mills, the river, or the moon, Bill relapsed into silence and walked down the platform. At the end he turned.

"God," he exclaimed (most of Bill's sentences began that way), "there's a light in the boss's window. He must have gone to bed and forgot it."

Bill went down the road and knocked at the office door.

"Come," cried some one inside, and Bill opened the door.

"Ah, Bill," said the superintendent, "is that you? I was just going over to see you. Young Mr. Watkins, the president's son, is coming down with a private car on the eleven four. His car will be cut out here and will go on the switch. It's all clear, is it not?"

"Yes," said Bill, "the switch is clear, but why is he comin' here? Aint Kalamazoo good enough fer him?"

The superintendent smiled. "Why are *you* here, Bill?"

"'Cause I aint never had money enough to git away," replied Bill; and then, realizing that his sentence was incomplete, he added, after an interval, "God."

"I wonder why *I* am here," said the superintendent, musingly. "I have a smattering of Latin and Greek. I speak French and Spanish, and I am not entirely unacquainted with Shakespeare and the musical glasses—when they are full—and yet here I am."

They sat gazing into the fire, thinking of very different things, when there came, floating up the valley, the whistle of the eleven four. The superintendent lit a lantern and the two went out, up the road, across the tracks, and stood upon the platform.

Far down in the west they saw a light that, as they watched it, grew larger and brighter. Soon they felt, rather than heard, a humming in the air. The blur of sound resolved itself into a rhythmic beat, and then lost itself in a roar. The light spread and tipped the black forest on either side; a white jet of steam shot up from the glare; two shrill whistles set the echoes flying; the great, hot, panting engine staggered past them, and with groaning brakes the eleven four arrived on time.

The conductor jumped from the forward platform.

"Bill," he said, "we 've got a private on the end. I 'll run ahead and kick it back. All clear?"

"Yes," said Bill. "Who 's 'lected?"

"Did n't hear," replied the conductor. "Mighty close, but reckon it 's Bryan."

"God," said Bill, "that 's two dollars for one. P'r'aps I kin git away from here now."

[186]

When the private car came back on the switch, the superintendent stood at its steps with his lantern. Soon the door opened and a boy in knickerbockers came out. He was tall and ruddy and smiling.

"Is this Catamount?" he asked.

"It is," replied the superintendent. "You are Mr. Watkins, are you not?"

"Well," said the boy, "I am Tom Watkins. *Mr.* Watkins is in Kalamazoo. I'm nothing but his son. I've come down here to learn the business and grow up with the country. Hello," he exclaimed, as the lantern shone on the face of the superintendent. "You are Mr. Blount, aint you? My father told me about you. You are an Oxford man. Come on board. I'm in disgrace, you know. Sent down here on account of a little trouble I had at Harvard. The dean is very fussy. I've got my luggage, my man, a bike, and two dogs aboard. Shall I get off, or spend the night in the car? It goes back in the morning."

"I think," said Blount, as he seated himself upon the piano-stool in the parlor

[187]

of the car, "that you will be more comfortable here, perhaps. I have had a bed put up for you in a room over the office, and Mrs. Brice will see that you get something to eat. She keeps the boarding-house for the head men. Let me suggest that you do not overlook Mrs. Brice. She is a social leader here. She wears shirt-waists, and she plays the melodeon when a preacher comes this way."

Tom Watkins laughed and then he winked.

"Thank you for the steer," he said. "I 'll attend to Mrs. B. the first thing in the morning. I 'll get her over before the car leaves and have her play the piano. This is the only car the Pullmans have with a piano. It was fitted up for travelling opera troupes, so they could practise between stands. My man hits the box in great shape. He 's been playing and singing for me all the way down from Columbus. If you say so, I 'll have him in. I should like to have you hear him sing, 'I want but little, but I want it nice.'

[188]

It's great. He can do all the music-hall stunts. He only came over from London last spring. I got him settling up a poker debt with Russ Suffolk, just after the dean turned me down. Russ is a great swell in college. His people threw the tea over in the war of 1812, or some of those scraps. Russ used to say to me, 'Tom, if your grandfather had made the money, instead of your father, you would n't be impossible'; and then he'd borrow a hundred and go off to the club. When the dean turned me down, Russ came in to see me. 'Old man,' he said, 'I owe you four hundred, and I owe my man the same. He's an invaluable man. He valeted Lord Oldcastle when he went on the special mission to Berlin about that ruby that was taken off the Prince at the masquerade; and he was in the bushes when Captain O'Kelly fought the duel with the Grand Duke at Boulogne, and he helped carry the Duke to the carriage after it was over. If you take a man like that back to Kalamazoo, Tom, you'll paralyze the

town. Now, I'll tell you what we'll do.
We'll have just one poker hand, with a
draw. If you win, you take Dawson, pay
him the four hundred I owe him and can-
cel my debt to you. If you lose, you take
Dawson and I continue to owe you each
four hundred.' We dealt the cards and
Russ drew three. I held up a pair and
drew three. On the show-down I had my
pair and Russ had nothing.

"'You win,' he said, 'and I'll send
Dawson over. Good-by, old man.'

"When he had gone, I looked at his
discard. He had thrown away three jacks.
Some of those old families are no fools."

Blount looked hard at his companion
and then said, "May I ask your age, Mr.
Watkins?"

The boy started, blushed to his hair,
and then sprang up and began to pace the
floor.

"I beg your pardon," said Blount. "I
have been down here so long that I am
off in my manners."

"No," exclaimed the boy, stopping before the man, "I know I am a fool. I know I have no chance with men like you. But think of it. I never knew my mother, and my father got his start filing saws in the lumber mills. He has made money. He is one of the richest men in Michigan, and he sent me to college to learn to be a gentleman, and what did he give me to start with? A check-book."

Now it was the man who blushed.

"Tom," he said, and the boy flushed again, but this time it was with pleasure, "I carried to Oxford much more than you took to Harvard, and I brought less away. You must not think hard of your father. It is better to begin by filing saws and end a man of power, than to begin with power and end by filing saws."

"Father *told* me," said the boy, "that you were a gentleman."

The Englishman drew himself up and bowed stiffly. "Approbation from Sir Hubert Stanley—" he began, then he laughed and took up his lantern. "Good night," he said. "I invite myself to breakfast with you in the morning." He turned at the end of the car. "By the way," he drawled, "if I may presume so far, I would suggest that you let Dawson go back to Kalamazoo. There is absolutely no society for him here. He would be desolated."

When his guest had departed, the boy pressed the button of the electric bell.

Dawson came in from the end of the car.

"Dawson," said the boy, "did you see my friend Mr. Blount?"

Dawson stood irresolute.

"Why don't you answer?" asked the boy, sharply.

"Beg pardon, sir," said Dawson, "but do you mean the gentleman that just went out, sir?"

Something in Dawson's voice caused the boy to look up.

"What are you fidgeting about?" he asked. "Do you know him?"

"The gentleman that just went out, sir," said Dawson, slowly, "is the Honorable Gerald Fitzallen, the youngest son of the Earl of Oldcastle. I packed his boxes, sir, when they sent him down from Christchurch. It broke his lordship's heart, sir."

"Dawson," said the boy, after a pause, "you may go back in the car to-morrow, and don't let Mr. Blount see you before you go. It might be uncomfortable for him. Call me at eight, and tell the cook to have breakfast on the table at half-past. That's all."

"I quite understand, sir," said Dawson. "Good night, sir."

The next morning Blount and the boy had their breakfast in the car, and when they had finished, Mrs. Brice came over from the boarding-house to try the piano. She wore her very best shirt-waist and was, perhaps, overdressed. She began, timidly, with her show piece, and did not make an entire success of it, but the boy helped her.

"Mrs. Brice," he cried, clapping his hands, "you played that way up in G, but it is too classical for me. Give us something simple."

And Mrs. Brice, reassured, let her fingers wander among the keys, and out there came wonderful melodies, filled with sad minors and strange conceits, the songs that her mammy had sung to her long "before the war." When she had played for some time, she began to sing. All her embarrassment had left her. Her rich voice filled the narrow car and floated through the open windows across the river, where the hands in the lumber yards stopped their work to listen.

When the song ceased, Blount was staring hard at the ceiling, and there were tears in the boy's eyes.

"Thank you," he said, "I never heard anything like that before."

"It has done me good," said Mrs. Brice, "to get away from my oven and my wash-tubs for a little while, and now I must get back to them."

When she had gone, Blount and the boy went over to the office, where they found a crowd of head men waiting to be presented to the son of the president.

The boy was somewhat awed by the thought that all these men were working for his father, and that some day they would be working for him.

"What are those rifles for?" he asked, pointing to a rack against the wall.

Blount laughed. "Have you never heard of the Hatfields and the McCoys?" he asked.

"Yes," replied the boy, "they are the families that have the feud and are always killing each other, are n't they?"

"Yes," said Blount, "and we have thirty of them out in the yards piling lumber. When we opened the mill they used to carry their Winchesters all day and work with one hand. We paid them for half a day's work. Last month I made a rule that no man should carry a gun into the yards, and they had a caucus and agreed. They come here in the morning, leave their Winchesters, get checks for them, and reclaim them at the end of the day. We pay them full wages now."

"This place is quite different from Cambridge, is n't it?" said the boy. "And even from Kalamazoo," he added.

"Yes," said Blount, "it is older. The men who live in these mountains are nearly the best bred men in the States. I am speaking as an Englishman now, and I mean that they are the descendants of younger sons who were driven out of Old Virginia. Their ancestors came here for cause, and they have bred true. They have handed down lawlessness and pride of birth."

"It seems to me," said the boy, "that Kalamazoo is the place for me. I ran up against pride of birth at Cambridge, and now I run up against it in Catamount. I thought I should be 'good people' here."

"The place for you," said Blount, "is New York. Several old families have started there since I have been in the States."

The door opened and a man came into the office. He was tall, but his shoulders dragged. His hair was long, unkempt,

[196]

and the color of flax. His beard was thin, and from the corners of his mouth two black lines ran part way down it. His eyes were china-blue and watery. He was dressed in butternut homespun. On his feet were a pair of low shoes, broken, and red with dried mud. He wore no stockings, and he carried a Winchester in the hollow of his left arm.

Blount rose and pushed out a chair.

"Ah, Mr. Dinwiddie," he said, "how are you? This is Mr. Watkins, from Michigan, the son of our president."

Mr. Dinwiddie slowly seated himself and planted the stock of his Winchester between his feet.

"Beg pardon," said Blount, pointing to the rifle, "but you know the rule of the office."

Dinwiddie slowly raised his weapon, threw open the breech, and held it up to show that it was empty. Then he handed it to Blount, who turned to the boy and showed him three notches cut in the grip of the stock.

[197]

"Those stand for the men he has killed," he whispered. "He's not much of a murderer. One of those in the rack has twenty-two notches. It belongs to Cy Hatfield. He holds the record. He has been tried for murder thirteen times, and the jury has always disagreed. He is out on bail now."

Blount handed the rifle back to its owner.

"All right, Mr. Dinwiddie," he said. "What can I do for you?"

"I come in this mornin'," said the man with three notches on his rifle, "to git a clothes-line. I toted in some corn, and they weighed it to the store, and it come to thirty-two cents, and the clothes-line is thirty-six. What be I goin' to do?"

"I shall esteem it a favor," said Blount, "if you will permit me to arrange it for you;" and he went out and returned with the line.

"Is that a swell?" asked the boy, when Dinwiddie had departed.

"If descent makes one," replied Blount, "he is. If ascent makes one, he is not. Take your choice."

They crossed the bridge to the great saw-mill. The boy stood entranced. For an hour he watched the dripping logs come slowly in the door, riding on an endless chain. He saw them seized with canthooks and rolled upon the carriage. He saw the "nigger-head" dart up through the floor, dash its sharp beak into the log, and fling it into position. He saw the head sawyer hold up his fingers to designate to the riders the thickness of the cut. He saw them set their gauge and their clamps. He saw the log borne down onto the great whirring, flashing bandsaw which sliced it as if it were cheese. He heard the rush of the returning carriage. He saw the white boards carried away in the distance, to be measured, sorted, piled on the trucks, and shot onto the long scaffolding which zigzagged up the valley for half a mile. They went to the dry-kilns, where great piles of lumber lay seasoning. They went to the huge stack, where the sawdust, that would otherwise swamp the mill, was burning with a roar like Niagara. They went to the planing-mill, where small machines cut up and smoothed strips of oak for parquette flooring. So deft, ingenious, and perfect was the work that the boy laughed aloud as he watched.

"Thunder!" he said, "those machines are alive. I feel like asking them questions."

"There is only one thing they cannot do," said Blount, "they cannot sort the strips according to color. That must be done by the human eye and hand."

They crossed the bridge again, and at the repair shop Blount spoke to a man in blue overalls who was wiping his blackened hands on a bunch of waste.

"Is steam on No. 3?"

"Yes, sir," replied the man.

"Run her out," said Blount, "and couple on a flat. Put some soap boxes on for seats, and run us up to the camps."

"It is rather nice," said the boy, "to order out a special train like that."

They reached the camp at the noon hour, and they dined in the boarding-house, Blount at the head of the table and the camp boss and the boy at his either hand. The latter wondered at the amount of pie consumed, and spoke of it.

"Ah," said Blount, "the more one lives out of doors the more he craves sweets. If a man in the camp here steals anything it is sure to be sugar. A *pâté de foie gras* would be perfectly safe."

After dinner they went out with the cutters and watched the great trees tremble, rock, and then, with a mighty rush of wind, come sweeping to the earth. Sometimes, as the last ligaments parted, the dying giants shrieked as they fell.

"I don't like this," said the boy. "It is too much like homicide."

"I have never grown quite used to it," said Blount. "Suppose we go back."

"Is this the end of the road?" asked the boy.

"Yes," replied his companion, "we extend it as we cut."

"I believe I will walk on a bit," said the boy.

"Very good," said Blount. "Follow the valley, and you will come to a trail on the left. It goes on forever. When you have had enough, come back here and take any train. I must go to the office."

When the boy had gone up the bank of the stream for a half-mile, he found the trail and turned into it. It was two feet wide and twisted through the forest, a faint line on the dark carpet of fallen leaves. The sunlight was shaded by the tree-tops, and the great trunks marked out the aisles and transepts of the first temple. There was no sound. The small, brown birds that flitted about the path were mute. The silence awed the boy, and he went on slowly. Suddenly he stopped. At his feet, lying across the path, was a green branch, freshly broken.

"How did that come here?" he asked himself. He picked it up. It was laurel,

[202]

and there was none growing in sight. He went on a little further, and there was another branch across the trail. He looked about, and far ahead he caught a glimpse of bright color that instantly disappeared. He went on faster, passing branch after branch. Finally he stopped and picked up another, that lay at the foot of a gigantic poplar, fifteen feet in girth. As he stood, perplexed, he heard a low but merry laugh. He stepped around the tree-trunk and came upon a girl who wore a pink cotton dress, and who held in her arms a bunch of laurel twigs.

The boy, being a boy, blushed, and took off his cap; and the girl, being a girl, laughed. Then the boy laughed too. The sombre forest suddenly became a very pleasant place. When it seemed silly to laugh any longer, the boy began to cast about for something to say. He was so long about it that the girl spoke first.

"Where is your bottle?" she asked.

"My bottle?" said the boy. "I haven't any."

[203]

The girl laughed again. She did not giggle, nor guffaw. She laughed with the silvery gurgle of a brook running over pebbles, and when she laughed the boy saw that there were dimples in her glowing cheeks, her dainty chin, and at the corners of her red lips.

"If you haven't got a bottle," she said, "why did you take up the twig?"

"I don't know," replied the boy. "I saw it in the path and wondered how it got there. What does it mean? Why did you put it there?"

"You don't know much, do you?" asked the girl.

"No," said the boy, "I've never had a chance."

"Well," resumed the girl, "father ran his still last night and made between four and five gallons. The twigs mean that if you leave your bottle and your money opposite one of them, you will find your bottle full in the morning."

"Ah," said the boy, "I understand—moonshine?"

"Yes," said the girl. "We have to live. Good-by."

"Where are you going?" asked the boy.

"Home," replied the girl, pointing up the trail.

"May I go with you?" he asked.

"Sure," she answered, "the road is free."

They walked on, saying little; and soon they came to the creek, clear and ankle deep at the edge, but dark and strewn with bowlders in the channel.

"You'd better take off your shoes and stockings," said the girl.

The boy looked down at his companion's feet. They were bare, but she was not ashamed. She led the way, leaping from stone to stone with her bare feet, and the boy followed as best he could in his Thomas golf shoes.

Watching the girl, he made a miss of the centre stone, and laughing, he slipped into the waist-deep water. She heard the splash, and leaping back, gave him her hand. He grasped it, and it was so strong but yet so soft, so warm, so vital, that he could not bear to let it go; so he held it until they reached the other side, and even then, he kept it and stood looking into her face. As he gazed at her he saw her eyes grow soft and then droop. He saw the rich blood come rushing into her cheeks, and then, being a boy, and she being a girl, he felt his heart stop beating, and bending down, he kissed her.

. . . .

When they came back to earth and felt the sunshine and heard the whispering of the leaves and the singing of the stream, the girl exercised the prerogative of her sex, and again spoke first.

"Are you my lover?" she asked.

"Yes," replied the boy, "I am your lover."

"Do you mean true?" she said, her hands on his shoulders, her eyes searching his.

"Yes," said the boy, "I mean true;" and they went on up the trail, hand in hand.

They walked slowly, and being a boy and a girl, they stopped often, so that it was some time before they came to a little clearing, unfenced and dotted with tree-stumps, about which grew goldenrod and wild asters. In the centre stood a cabin built of hewn logs, their joints plastered with clay.

"There," said the girl, pointing toward the cabin, "that's my home."

The boy felt a bit queer, just then. He thought of his father's house in Kalamazoo, with its wooden towers and minarets, its *porte-cochère*, its great bare lawn with the tulip bed and the two green cast-iron settees in the centre, and for a brief moment he speculated as to how the president would regard this first afternoon spent in Catamount.

Soon, however, he was thinking of other things, for as they approached the cabin, a man came out and stood before the door. He was tall, but bent; his hair was flaxen and touched his shoulders, and from the corners of his mouth two black

[207]

stains ran down his beard. He was dressed in butternut, and he carried a Winchester in the hollow of his left arm. His eyes were china-blue.

"Dinwiddie?" exclaimed the boy.

"Yes," said the girl; and then as they came up to the door she said, "Father, this is my lover."

There followed a silence that the boy thought would never end. It ended with a click. Dinwiddie had cocked his rifle. The boy began to think again of his father and of Kalamazoo. He did not look at the girl; he kept his eyes on the gun, or perhaps on the man behind the gun.

"Rosie," said the man with the china-blue eyes,—and his voice was low and sweet, like the girl's,—"they ain't none better born nor you in all the mountings. You're Dinwiddie on yer pa's side, and yer ma had Pocahonty blood. Bein' bred like that, it would n't be right fer you to cross with no galoot from Michi*gan*. No, no, Rosie; you kin do a heap better. Cy Hatfield is bailed out, I seen him at the mill. He's comin' up to-night and he's goin' to marry you to-morrer."

With a cry like a wild beast's, the girl sprang at her father and struck him in the face.

"Good," said Dinwiddie, calmly, as he drew his sleeve across his cheek. "That Pocahonty blood is game. Yer ma had it."

Then he straightened himself, and his china-blue eyes grew hard and evil.

"Go," he said to the boy, and he pointed toward the trail.

The boy hesitated.

"Shall I go, Rosie?" he asked.

"Yes," sobbed the girl. "He'll kill you if you don't."

"Go," repeated Dinwiddie, in a voice no longer low and sweet. "And don't yer come back again. If yer do, by God, there'll be four nicks on my gun 'stead of three."

II

THE next morning the boy came very late to his breakfast. Mrs. Brice waited for him and was embarrassed and distressed by his want of appetite. She even suggested some dried-apple pie. When a man in Catamount starts in to drink, because he is paid off, or has had a baby born, or a funeral in his family, he is apt to have pie for breakfast. Just so the man who has been fortunate in "the Street" eats melons at the Waldorf in February. The boy declined the pie, drank a little tea, nibbled a slice of toast, and pushed back his chair.

Outside the sun was shining as usual; the sluggish river eddied by the booms, the air was filled with the hum of the band-saws, the clack of the planers, the puffing of the logging locomotives, the roar of the sawdust-burner.

The boy went slowly down the road, crossed the railway, and passed on to the store. He did not enter, but stood upon the steps, his hands in his coat pockets, his thoughts far up the trail.

Suddenly he heard a clatter on the bridge. He looked and saw a gray mule

shacking down the road. On her back was
a slouching rider clad in butternut. The
sun glistened on the barrel of a rifle.

"Dinwiddie!" gasped the boy. And
then he set his teeth and stood his ground.

The gray mule came on and finally
stopped before the store. The rider swung
his right leg and dismounted slowly. He
threw his reins over the mule's head upon
the ground. Then he came up the steps.

"Mornin'," he said. "How be ye?"

The boy stood silent.

"They's goin' to be a weddin' at our
house to-night," said the man with the
china-blue eyes, "and I come in to git a
few fixin's. I haint got no ready money,
and what be I goin' to do?"

The boy led the way into the store.

"Mr. Barton," he said to the clerk,
"let Mr. Dinwiddie have what he wants
and charge it to me."

With the bazaars of the world before
him, Mr. Dinwiddie chose two pairs of
ladies' white cotton hose, one pair of gents'
ditto; one pair of ladies' shoes, No. 3,

[211]

one pair of gents' ditto, No. 10; six cotton pocket-handkerchiefs, one celluloid comb, a pound of cheese, and twenty-five Winchester cartridges.

"There," he said, when he had completed his purchases, and was about to remount his mule, "fer clost on to two hundred year my fambly has been married in shoes and stockin's. I must be goin'. Cy and Rosie is down the trail, fillin' the bottles and takin' up the money." He kicked his mule and started, only to wheel about and return.

"Mr. Watkins," he said, "no hard feelin's 'twixt us, be they? We could n't quite 'low you to marry inter the fambly, but we'll keep on tradin' to your store jist the same."

He started again and wheeled again.

"Mr. Watkins," he said, restraining his restive mule, "Rosie says, 'Tell Tom, if you sees him, to come up the trail some time when Cy's in jail.'"

THE EYE
OF THE HAREM

THE EYE
OF THE HAREM

WHEN the Bishop had passed the customs—a High Church inspector letting certain embroidered vestments through as "tools to be used in a trade," under Schedule Z—he took a cab and had his wife and himself driven to the Albemarle. His rooms were ready for him, and his letters were on a table in the sitting-room. His wife, a small, thin woman with gray hair drawn over her ears, examined the letters and selected her own. Then she permitted the Bishop to have his. He went into his chamber, and soon came to the door in his shirt-sleeves.

"Maria," he called, "here is a note from Tewksbury. An engagement prevented his meeting us at the wharf, but he puts his carriage at our disposal while we are here, sends his kindest remembrances to you and incloses—"

[215]

"What?" asked his wife, with a hair-pin in her mouth.

"Nothing," replied the Bishop, "that is," he added, "only a card;" and having been so near to an untruth, he thought of Saint Peter and half listened for the cock's crow.

"Well," said his wife, after a short interval, her mouth still occupied by the necessaries of her toilet, "if I felt equal to it I should go around to Trinity Chapel and give thanks for a safe voyage, but my head is very bad and I shall try to sleep. Of course you will go."

There was a knock at the door. The Bishop went to it hurriedly.

"Please, sir," said the buttons, "Mr. Tewksbury's carriage is below, and the groom says he is to take your orders."

The Bishop went to the door of his wife's room.

"My dear," he said, "I wish I could do something for you. I don't like to leave you alone."

"Nonsense," rejoined his wife, "it

won't be the first time. There is a little
foreign money in my purse. Put it in the
offertory, I dare say they can use it, and
get me some fruit while you are out—
that nasty steamer food! lobsters on the
menu six days out!—get me some nectarines, such as we had at Lambeth Palace;
there is a fruit-shop just up the street;
and don't wake me up to show them to
me. Wait till I call you."

"Yes, my dear," said the Bishop, and
he went down-stairs and entered the neat
brougham which stood before the door.

"Where, my lord?" asked the footman.

"Anywhere," sighed the Bishop as he
sank back against the cushions.

They drove through the park, and the
sweetness of the landscape brought peace
to the Bishop's heart.

"After all," he said to himself, "a celi-
bate clergy has its limitations. See those
baby-carriages and white-capped nurses
on the lawn. None of them, it is to be
hoped, belongs to the Pope, and any one

of them — in fact, all of them — might belong to my humblest curate. Then, there is the question of stockings. Maria keeps mine darned. Friars are barefooted, doubtless because they have no one to darn for them. By the way, what was it Maria told me to fetch her? Oh, nectarines, that's it. I've plenty of time and will get them after I have let the carriage go," and just then they quitted the macadam of the park for the asphalt of the avenue.

In a few moments the Bishop, who had been watching the street-lamps, squeezed the rubber bulb which hung in front of the brougham door, and the coachman drew up to the left-hand curb.

The Bishop backed slowly out, one foot on the step and the other feeling for the sidewalk.

"James," he said, when he had found his legs — and very good legs they were in their gaiters — "James, that is all."

"Thank you, my lord," said James, raising his forefinger to his hat-brim.

"And, James," added the Bishop, "if

any one should ask where you left me, you may say at the corner of Thirty-eighth Street. This *is* the corner of Thirty-eighth Street, is it not?"

"Quite so, my lord," replied James.

"I have enjoyed my drive very much," said the Bishop. "Share this with the coachman," and he slipped his wife's foreign money, wrapped in a bill, into James's hand.

The Bishop stood a moment, as if undecided where to go, then he walked briskly down the avenue. As he went along men and women turned to look at him, the men a little slyly, the women with frank admiration. Miss Dottie St. Claire, who was driving home from rehearsal, put her blond head out of the hansom and gazed after him.

"Aren't he a love?" she said to the young man by her side. "He makes me think of 'ome."

And the Bishop was well worth looking at. Six feet tall, with a smooth, ruddy face, kind blue eyes, crisp gray hair under a shovel hat, neat gaiters, well-blackened boots, and just enough waist to show off his apron, he was a pleasing object,— so pleasing, indeed, that it was difficult for certain lewd men who passed him to conceive that he was the direct descendant of the apostles, who, they whispered one to another, were simple folk, with only one coat, one pair of shoes, and no stockings, no gaiters, no amethyst episcopal rings, no broughams, and no incomes.

But the good Bishop, as he walked down the avenue, was not troubled by these aspersions of his legitimacy. His thoughts were evidently fixed on pleasanter things than the bar sinister with which envy sought to daub his sacerdotal escutcheon.

"I wonder," he said to himself, "if this is the place?" and he stopped and looked up at a corner house.

"Yes," he said, consulting a card which he held in his hand; "this is the number, but it might be a private house for all that appears. I had supposed—" and then he went up the steps which were on the side street and touched the bell. The door opened instantly.

"Is this the Saunterers' Club?" he asked of the servant who stood on the threshold.

"Yes, my lord," replied the hallman.

The Bishop blushed, first with pleasure, and again because his conscience pricked him.

"I am Bishop Williamson, of Porto Rico," he said, "and I received notice to-day that my old friend, Mr. Robert Tewksbury, has obtained the privileges of this club for me for two weeks. Is Mr. Tewksbury in?" and he held out the card.

"No, my lord," replied the doorman, "but he will be, later. He telephoned for dinner only a few moments ago."

The Bishop went in and a servant took his hat.

"I will show you about the 'ouse, my lord," he said.

The Bishop blushed again. He found

[221]

it pleasant to be addressed by English servants.

They entered the library.

"Ah!" exclaimed the Bishop, "this is delightful. Such quiet, such repose, such a refuge from the hurly-burly of the street! I think I will try one of these hospitable chairs."

"Shall I bring you a paper, my lord?" asked the servant.

"Yes," replied the Bishop. "I should like to see the last copy of the *Churchman*."

"Very sorry, my lord, but we don't take in the *Churchman*," said William. "Will you try the *Evening Post*, my lord? The *Post* is a very serious paper."

"No," replied the Bishop. "I think I will take a little rest. I have had a busy day. And, by the way," he added, his conscience pricking him again, "I am not 'my lord.' I am simply Bishop Williamson, of Porto Rico."

"Thank you, my lord," said William; and then he went away.

Left to himself, the good Bishop glanced languidly about the room,—its huge chairs, heavy curtains, sombre color, and subdued lights, so inviting to repose. Then, assured that he was alone, he stretched out his gaitered legs, crossed his white hands over his apron, dropped his chin upon his breast, and slept.

He had scarcely lost himself when the clear notes of a coach-horn filled the room. It was evidently blown at the club door. The Bishop awakened with a jerk, and getting on his feet, walked to the open window. He was just in time to see a black drag, picked out in yellow, draw up to the curb. While it was still in motion two servants ran to the heads of the horses, and when the brake was set a tall man in a drab coat, who was sitting on the box seat, threw the reins onto the wheelers' backs and stood up. The horses spread their legs and breathed hard. It was evident that they had come fast. A crowd gathered instantly from the place from which crowds come, and men with

bare heads ran out of the club and stood
about the front wheels.

"Good old Tewksbury," cried some
one from the club steps.

"Good old Macaroni," cried another.

"Three cheers for Spaghetti," yelled a
third, and they were given with a will.

"Gentlemen," said Tewksbury, brac-
ing himself on the footboard, "the filly
ran true to breeding, and there will be
cakes and ale in the blue dining-room
at eight o'clock. I hope you all landed
well. You haven't time to go home and
dress. Come as you are. All you need is a
thirst."

"Bless me," said the Bishop, to himself, "can that man in those very pronounced clothes be Robert Tewksbury?
When I last saw him, at the General
Convention"—and then the door flew
open and Tewksbury came in.

"David, old boy, how are you?" he
cried.

"Bob," replied the Bishop, "I am very
well."

The two men stood gazing and smiling at each other.

"You old sinner," said Tewksbury, "how your togs become you!"

"You old saint," said the Bishop, "how funny you look in yours!" and then they laughed and shook hands for a long time.

"I saw your arrival in the *Herald*," said Tewksbury, "and I sent my coachman round to you with the carriage. Did he find you?"

"Indeed he did," said the Bishop, "and I got your card for the club, and came to thank you. I have to choose my time, for we are very busy, and Maria is a little nervous."

"How *is* Maria?" asked Tewksbury.

"Just as ever," replied the Bishop, "as true as steel."

"Humph," said Tewksbury.

The Bishop sighed.

As the mention of his wife had caused the silence which ensued, he felt bound to break it.

"What have you been doing lately, Bob?" he asked.

"Doing?" exclaimed Tewksbury,—"everything. This has been my busy year. I went to Europe last October, fell in with the Turkish ambassador at London, went on with him to Constantinople, worked out a loan for the Sultan, cleaned up a million, came home last week, and to-day I won the 'Far and Near' with my filly Spaghetti, by Macaroni, out of Vermicelli."

"What is the 'Far and Near'?" asked the Bishop.

Tewksbury looked hard at his friend.

"Dave," he said, finally, "you always were rather downy at school. You used to pretend ignorance of lots of things with which you had at least a bowing acquaintance. This supposed ignorance of yours went far toward making you a bishop."

The Bishop smiled a sort of smile, but he asked again, "What is the 'Far and Near'?"

[226]

"If you're honest about it," said Tewksbury, "it's a horse-race, and I won it to-day, along with forty thousand dollars, and I'll build you a chapel in Porto Rico if you'll dine with me to-night." He was evidently somewhat excited.

The Bishop sat silent for a moment, and then he uttered the single word, "Maria?"

"Be a man, Dave," said Tewksbury.

The Bishop's hands clasped the arms of his chair, and the charming bow of his lips became a straight line.

"Bob," he said, "I will."

"Good," exclaimed Tewksbury, "the chapel is yours."

"I'm afraid," said the Bishop, "that I should have stayed without the chapel. I am periodically attacked with a longing to mingle with my fellow-men. Thus far I have fought against it, although in London I fell, and went to Madame Tussaud's. But to-day I have scarcely struggled. I started out this afternoon with the deliberate intention of coming here. I dismissed your carriage at the corner of Thirty-eighth Street, and told James to say he had set me down there. I thought it would not look well if I drove up to the door of a club, and I proposed to say nothing about it to Maria. This is bad enough, but it is not the worst, for, Bob, I actually revel in the deceit. I am wildly happy in my sin, and I propose to quaff the cup of pleasure to the dregs; but, Bob," he added earnestly, "you must let me know when it is ten o'clock. Till then I shall be a man among men. After ten, I shall be the Bishop of Porto Rico, and shall go home to Maria. I know what you are going to say. You are about to suggest that I tell Maria that I stayed out in order to get the chapel. There are two objections to that. One is that it is not true, and the other is that Maria will know that it is not true. By the way, I left her to go to Trinity Chapel, and then to get her some nectarines at Hick's. Don't let me forget them."

"All right," said Tewksbury, "you

have plenty of time to run over to the Albemarle and tell her you are going to dine with me."

" By no means," exclaimed the Bishop. " I shall send a note. I am not Catiline. If I go, I shall not return."

"All right," laughed Tewksbury. "You know best. I 'll just run upstairs and do a tub. I sha' n't change because the others have n't time. By the way, what clothes do you wear at coronations and such like ? "

The Bishop blushed for the third time.

" When I dined at Lambeth Palace," he said, " I wore silk stockings and silver buckles on my pumps, but my coat was very like the one I have on, except that it was braided."

" You 'll do above the waist, then," said Tewksbury, " and your legs will be under the table. Come along if you want to wash your hands."

II

A SCORE of men sat about the long table in the blue room. There were bank-

[229]

ers, railroad presidents, promoters, corporation lawyers, idlers; all were millionnaires except the Bishop and a little man in tweeds who sat at the host's left. The little man was presented to the Bishop by Tewksbury as his trainer; "and what Jenkins does n't know about horses," he added, "you can put in tea."

"How very interesting," rejoined the Bishop. "I should enjoy a long talk with you, Mr. Jenkins, about that noblest of animals, the horse. You doubtless recall the matchless description of him in the Book of Job."

"I carnt say as I do, my lord," replied Mr. Jenkins. "What with lookin' after three and thirty in trainin', keepin' the stable lads sober, warnin' off the touts and reporters, seein' after the weights and entries, nursin' the sick ones, patchin' up the cripples, takin' off my 'at to the jocks, as you has to do now-a-days, and with oats at forty-eight cents, I don't have the time for much readin', but I was well acquainted with Job."

"What?" exclaimed the Bishop.

"Of course you understand," added Mr. Jenkins, "that Job was n't his real name. He just took it for sportin' purposes, and he used to sign it to the racin' articles in the *Spirit*. He called on me once at the stables, a proper gentleman with sandy hair and a blue bird's-eye tie —did n't ask for no tips—just passed the time of day—gave me a cigar—had the clothes off of Macaroni—went into the 'ouse to see the picture of the old 'orse with me at his 'ead—took a cup of tea with the missus—liked to killed her with one of his stories—'ad the little girl onto his lap, and went away as pleasant as a May mornin'. I 'll look up his book this winter unless we take the string South."

"I fear," said the Bishop, "that I did not make myself quite clear. I had reference to—"

"David," interrupted Tewksbury, "do you see that lad down at the other end, the chap with the white hyacinth in his buttonhole? He is Carrol De Lancy,

[231]

one of our most eminent cotillion leaders."

"Dear me," said the Bishop, "I have never seen one." After a look through his glasses, he turned to Tewksbury, his eyes twinkling, and whispered, "And a little child shall lead them."

"Not such a child as he looks," said Tewksbury. "He'll be presented to you later, and will ask you for the loan of his cab fare. He never carries any money in his evening clothes. Says it bulges him and spoils his figure. He's got a flat latchkey which he keeps in his hat lining. He gets his corsets from Klob in Vienna, who makes for the Pope's guard. They are the best set up chaps in Europe, bar none ; and the reason is that their corsets are made in one piece of elastic, which goes on over the head. It takes two men to put 'em on, and they say they are never taken off."

"Dear me," said the Bishop, "I had no idea—who is that man with the side whiskers, the one speaking to the waiter?"

"Oh," replied Tewksbury, "that's Jamieson, the most awful millionnaire here. He's drunk half that bottle, and now he is telling the waiter that it is corked. That's a habit. He paid a thousand dollars the other day to become a life member of the club. He immediately began to think. 'If I die inside of five years,' he said to me, 'my estate will lose money, as the annual dues are two hundred. What would you do?'

"I couldn't advise him. Later he came to me radiant.

"'I've fixed that matter I was speaking to you about,' he said. 'I've taken out a five-year policy on my life for a thousand dollars. My estate can't lose much. One has to look after these things.'"

"Dear me," said the Bishop, again. "I had no idea—and he is of a very old family, is he not?"

"I should say so," replied Tewksbury. "Good old Bible family. A lot of his ancestors ran violently down a steep place into the sea, and—"

"Tewksbury," called a man from the other end of the table, "they say that when you were in Turkey last winter the Sultan got sweet on you and gave you the Eye of the Harem. Can't we have a look at it, or have you locked it up in some safe deposit vault down town?"

"No," said Tewksbury, "I wore it to the races to-day, for luck, and I am ashamed to say, I have got it on yet," and he took off his ring and passed it on — a blue diamond as large as a filbert, with pink and white flashes through it that made the millionnaires gasp. To the Bishop it was only something to marvel at and admire; to the others, it was something to covet and appraise.

"A hundred thousand dollars, if it is worth anything," whispered the Bishop's right-hand neighbor. "Such jewels should be suppressed. They breed crime. They make thieves and poisoners. How often do you suppose blood has been spilled on account of that stone?"

The Bishop did not reply, for just then

[234]

a servant offered him a huge bowl of white and black grapes, and, as he helped himself to a small cluster, he uncovered a crimson-cheeked nectarine. He had forgotten his wife's commission.

"Are you ill?" asked his neighbor. "You look rather white. Let me get you some brandy."

"No," said the Bishop, with a faint smile, "it is my conscience, not my stomach, that is troubling me. I have thought too much of my own pleasure to-day, and too little of that of others. Now I must go and confess;" and he rose from his chair.

"Not going, are you, David?" asked Tewksbury.

"Yes," said the Bishop, "I must say good night."

"Well," said Tewksbury, "I'll see you out, and if no one will have any more drink, we will have our coffee in the other room. By the way, where is my ring?" and he held up the hand upon which he had worn it.

There followed a moment's silence and

then — " I passed it on," said one, "and
I," "and I," said each. They shook the
napkins and searched the floor. The cotillion leader took one of the candles
and disappeared under the table. No diamond. "Never mind," said Tewksbury,
"it will turn up all right. Don't think
any more about it."

Then they thought about it very hard
indeed, and a silence ensued that became
embarrassing. It was broken by Jamieson, the multi-millionnaire, who walked
unsteadily but rapidly to the door and
locked it.

"I move we all be searched," he cried,
in a voice made strident by drink. "I
can't afford to have diamonds like that
disappear at dinner-tables where I am.
Search me first and let me get out. Who's
next?"

"Mr. Jamieson," said Tewksbury,
"you forget yourself. These are my
guests. I don't have guests that have to
be searched."

"You've got nothing to do with it,"

screamed Jamieson. "It is a measure of self-preservation for each of us. We can't go until the stone is found, or until it is proved that we have n't got it. Do you all agree?"

And they all agreed but one—the Bishop. He stood, very erect and very pale, his hand extended to Tewksbury.

"I think I'll go now, Robert," he said, and then he turned and, looking down the room, added, "Good night, gentlemen."

There were a few awkward responses as Tewksbury unlocked the door and went out with his friend. The two did not speak until they stood on the steps of the club. Then Tewksbury put his hand on the Bishop's shoulder, and said, "Dave, it was awfully square of you to stand up and refuse to be searched. That drunken fool, Jamieson, put you all in a dreadful hole, and I know how hard it was for you to walk out. You did it for my sake."

"No, Bob," said the Bishop, sadly, "I did it for my own sake. I did n't dare to be searched. I am a thief."

[237]

"My God, Dave, what do you mean?" gasped Tewksbury.

"I mean," said the Bishop, "that I stole this," and putting his hand into his skirt pocket he drew out a nectarine.

Tewksbury glanced at it and burst into a laugh.

"It is no laughing matter," said the Bishop. "It made a sneak and coward of me. I had to run away or be exposed. Fancy an unworthy successor of the apostles searched, and found with stolen fruit on his person;" and drawing back his arm he flung the nectarine far down the street.

"Poor old boy," said Tewksbury, "I should not have asked you to such a dinner."

"It is not your fault," said the Bishop. "I deserve it all. I began the day wrong. I was not conscientious on the wharf this morning in regard to my vestments. And then I permitted Maria to believe that I left her to go to Trinity Chapel, and instead of going, I drove in the park. I gave her money to the groom when she had charged me to put it in the offertory. I wrote her that I was dining with you, but did not mention the club, and I forgot all about her fruit until that on your table reminded me of it. I am sorry that you have lost your ring, Bob, but I have lost much more—my self-respect."

"Nonsense," exclaimed Tewksbury. "You're morbid. You spend too much time with curates and women."

"I am going home to a woman now," said the Bishop, "and I am wondering just what I shall say to her. Good night," and he started down the street.

He walked very slowly, and he even took a little stroll in Madison Square before he entered the hotel. When he did go in, he declined the offer of the elevator and climbed the stairs. He opened the door very carefully and crept into the sitting-room. It was dark, but a faint glimmer of light came from his wife's room. He could hear her breathing. She was asleep. He was reprieved until morning. With a thankful heart he groped his way toward his own door. He had almost reached it when he stepped upon the projecting rocker of a chair. There was a bang against the wall, a cry from his wife, a sudden gleam of light as she turned up the gas, and then the Bishop of Porto Rico realized that his crimes had overtaken him.

He began to talk very rapidly: "Tewksbury asked particularly after you, my dear, —very particularly. We had a delightful dinner. I don't know when I have had so charming a dinner. We had oysters and soup and fish and roast and snipe— I think, yes, snipe—and, ha, ha, ha, there was a young man present who leads cotillions and wears corsets. It was a delightful dinner, most delightful—Tewksbury asked most particularly—"

"That will do," said his wife. "You may complete the menu in the morning. I wonder what they think down in the office of the Bishop of Porto Rico coming in at this hour of the night. Leave the nectarines in the sitting-room and go to bed." [240]

" My dear," began the Bishop, " I very much regret—"

There was a knock at the outer door. The Bishop answered it. A servant from the club stood in the hall with a small basket in his hand.

" My lord," he said, taking off his hat, " Mr. Tewksbury sends these nectarines with his compliments, and bids me say that he found the ring. He put it in his waistcoat pocket when it was passed back to him, and forgot all about it. Good night, my lord."

" Good night," said the Bishop, " and God bless you."

D. B. Updike
The Merrymount Press
Boston